March 23, 2014
To Margot and Steven —
I feel like I know you well,

Back Home in
Landing Run

Mary Popham

MOTES BOOKS

Back Home in Landing Run

Mary Popham

© 2013
All Rights Reserved.

FICTION
ISBN 978-1-934894-51-4

Copying this book is expressly forbidden according to copyright law.
No portion of this book may be copied, transmitted, duplicated,
stored or distributed in any form (including but not limited to
handwritten, photocopy, print, audio, video, digital or electronic)
without prior express written permission from the publisher,
with the sole exception of brief excerpts used in reviews or commentaries.

Cover Photo
Dr. Wanda J. Rogers

Book Design
EYE.*K*

Published in Kentucky by

www.MotesBooks.com

PRINTED & BOUND IN THE USA

for
Ronnie

Emmalene
March 1910

When Halley's Comet came through in May 1910 it made big news. Here in Landing Run, some said it was a sign of good things, like a great president being born, while others said it meant doomsday—floods and poison gas killing us all. Whichever it was, two months later Meadors Sawmill blew up and everything changed in our little community in central Kentucky, especially for me.

If the sawmill hadn't of blown up, then Dolin Linkahan wouldn't have needed a quiet place to get well—with me, Emmalene Hershall, as his nurse. And without Dolin at my house, then Les Richman wouldn't've come over ever day. Then he wouldn't've got a job working in my old husband's moonshine and I wouldn't be the cause of Les leaving Landing Run and, worse, of what happened to Old Man Hershall.

Sometimes I still go over how things came about. Being twenty years old and just married to a stooped, white-haired, eighty-four-year-old man was enough to set tongues a going. But what I didn't know was how much Landing Run people had against a Protestant.

It was back in March and the middle of the night when Mr. Hershall drove the buggy around a curved driveway and up to the front steps to his house—my new home.

Before we got to his farm in Nelson County, Mr. Hershall let me know there wasn't anybody would like me. "Except for me and mine, they's all Catlicks," he said. The fire in his eyes told me he hated Catholics, too. I didn't even know these people, and I could see I'd be lonesome, just like where I left.

"You're Emmalene Hershall now, and none of us Protestants is welcome here," said Mr. Hershall. "So don't be walking out to the store and smiling with your dimples and bright eyes, thinking to be neighborly, cause them idol worshippers ain't invited to my house, either!"

At the old man's warning, hope melted in my heart.

We had been on the road for two days and my hands and face stung from windburn. Most of the time, I held little Jakie in my lap, trying to keep us both warm. The old man's grandson never spoke, being a mute, but he leaned into me like he trusted me and it was the only thing that let me think I hadn't made a mistake by marrying and leaving the mountains of eastern Kentucky and my step-father's house. There was nothing else in my future except to get far away from my lost love, Jarboe Clemons. He told me he had got a girl in the family way and would be marrying her. It wasn't any way I could live near him anymore.

As we neared the farmhouse, I smelled manure on the crop beds that was ready for planting and saw moonlight flashing on the creek. The water curved to the left of the road, then went out of sight following the lowest places through the woods, then come back to the road again. I could tell from lantern lights in the distance that cabins and log houses was built in the uneven rise and fall of short hills, the knobs of Nelson County.

There wasn't any welcome to my new home from the old man when he stopped the buggy.

"You stay out here with the boy," said Mr. Hershall, "til I get the fire started." He wasn't tired out from the trip like I was. He walked bent-over, but I could tell he was strong and steady on his feet.

My new husband's voice was high and raspy and reminded me of the pet chicken I had when I was a little girl. It had got a twig stuck in its throat and after my mother pulled it out, the white bird squawked in a unnatural high pitch for the rest of its life.

I didn't answer Mr. Hershall, just nodded my head. The old man talked so gruff to me all the time, I never said much to him and he didn't act like he missed my conversation.

"Jakie, you're home," I said to the child. I thought he was asleep but even if awake, I was curious what all he understood. The little I knew about him was that he was ten-years old with the body and mind of one much younger. His mother had died at their mountain home, his father had gone crazy and nobody knew his whereabouts. Mr. Hershall had made the long trip from central Kentucky to get his grandson, and ended up getting me, too. I would be taking care of Jakie while Mr. Hershall went about his business. "He ain't right, you know," the old man had told me.

After lighting the fireplace logs, Mr. Hershall came back to the buggy. "Hand me the boy," he said and his high voice caught at me again. He left me to get my carpet bag of clothes and follow him inside. Jakie folded himself into his grandpaw's arms and rested his head on his shoulder. His skin was pale and his lashes dark, and he slept with his mouth open. I beheld peace in his face and contentment in the way he cuddled into the old man's arms. Even in sleep he seemed to know his place in the world, of belonging.

During the next couple of weeks I was relieved when Mr. Hershall stuck to the promise he made before I said I would marry him. "I am not taking you for a real wife. The first Miz Hershall what died years ago was my wife. You sleep in your bed and I sleep in mine!" I found out later where Mr. Hershall slept when he was indoors. It was a small room under the stair steps.

My room had nothing but a rickety bed for me and a new child's bed built in the wall alongside the fireplace for Jakie. Limp curtains was hung at the windows like clothes worn-out from hanging through untold rainy springtimes and dusty summers.

It didn't take nothing to learn where everything was kept and what to do for Jakie. The boy wasn't afraid of me, yet he didn't pay me too much mind. He ate what I fed him—mush for breakfast, beans and cornbread at dinner, a bigger meal at supper. He sat behind the warm stove in the kitchen, rocking his body back and forth and tapping a piece of tin with a wooden stick. Click-click, click-click, click-click. It became a happy sound, faster than the ticking clock on the mantel, but more of a comfort because it came from a living body besides myself.

Sometimes my hurting over Jarboe Clemons gave me reason to regret leaving my former home. But after thinking on it a while, I knew I was right to take my chances away from there. While I believed we would marry, he had betrayed me. Why would I want a husband I couldn't trust? Yet, how could I bear watching him with a wife that should have been me?

The old man told me right off, "People call me a hermit. They's right. I don't like being around nobody but my kin."

He kept his gold coins hid and wouldn't buy me nothing personal. "I'm laying out enough for you to get flour, salt and two or three scoops of sugar. You don't need ribbons and whatnots."

I had an idea to buy some little chicks, grow them into laying hens and sell the eggs at Rice's Store on Jackson Highway. Which Mr. Hershall said okay but I had to pay him back for the chickies. I laughed to myself at how stingy he was.

No doubt, he was mean-spirited to all but Jakie, yet I wished he would just pay me the kindness of some normal talk, even if it was about how the trees was budding out or if he thought the cow would drop her calf anyways soon, or if he liked how I cut Jakie's hair. But he just walked from the washpan at the back door to the kitchen table to his chair at the fireplace. And if I came to sit down with him, he'd go to his sleeping room or back outside. After Jakie was asleep, the most I heard was the throbbing of the tree frogs or the creak of my rocker.

Landing Run Road—really just a three-mile path of hard-packed dirt running along side the creek—was scarred with hoof prints and wheel ruts. It led out to Jackson Highway and Rice's Store was just to the left of the turn. There was no other store until Bardstown, six miles north.

In rainy weather, horses and buggies got muddy on our little community's road, but Landing Run Creek crossed it just before you made the turn onto Jackson Highway, which was a better road layered with heavy cobblestone and layers of smooth-rolled gravel over top. You might could stop at the creek and wash the horse's tail and your buggy wheels before you got to the crossroads, left to the store, or where the Catholics turned right to go to Our Lady of Hope Church.

Three miles was no piece at all when I took my first walk out to Rice's. I noted everything, marking old trees as guideposts. The short wooded hills around me were no match for the mountains and their saplings in the understory back home in Clay County, but they gave my heart a turn as they were studded with spring wildflowers—violets, white-flowered bloodroot and the spicebush shrub.

The general store was made of hand-hewed planks with notched corners like Mr. Hershall's farmhouse, and had a hitching bar between two posts right close to the highway. A U.S. flag hung from a front rafter showing it was a post office and old men sitting on the porch showed it was a gathering place. Will Miz Rice turn up her nose at me even though I live in a bigger house than the neighbors?

I needn't have worried. The tone of Miz Rice's voice told me she knew a paying customer. "Come on in, Girl. You sure are as pretty as a face on a cameo, just like ever body says!"

The first thing I thought was, Who told her that? Must be the neighbors are watching me when I don't even know it.

"I heard you walked all way here, today," she said.

Well, I wasn't going to be surprised any more at how much of my business everybody knew. Miz Rice made me a real good offer—she had a yard full of layers and would I take them off her hands. The hens wouldn't start up laying much eggs again til the end of March but I was happy to get them, as I wouldn't have to wait for chickies to grow up to start making money.

Emmalene
April 1910

I had been in Landing Run almost a month and I thought I'd never get to see Bardstown.

One morning in early April, Mr. Hershall said, "Get the boy ready. I got business at the courthouse."

I was excited as a kid. I put on my best dress, the dark rose-colored one with bows down the bodice. It had been Mother's but she hardly wore it any before she died. It was still too big in the waist for me but I had hemmed the skirt before I left the mountains. Nobody would see it under my coat anyway.

The only looking glass was beside the kitchen door and Mr. Hershall saw me brushing my hair. "Don't be fancying yourself up. You put a scarf on over them black curls. We're going to the courthouse, not to some dance."

I stared at him til he looked away and I went on brushing my hair. He gave me a short grunt and walked out of the room to get Jakie.

When the horse pulled from our lane and we turned onto Landing Run Road, I noticed two log houses settled across the way among the budding trees, each on top its own knob. They wasn't many leaves yet to hide the homes, and I saw each one plain and could picture what I knew about that kind of house. Both of them had two square log rooms with a built-in breezeway connecting them all under one roof. One side was mostly for cooking and the other side for living space and beds. A large stone chimney was at each outside end and upstairs would be holding more beds.

"Who lives there?" I asked Mr. Hershall.

"The Richmans on the closest knob and the Linkahans on the furtherest," he said. "They been here a hundred years but my daddy was here soon after that, so's they need not think they's the big cheese."

I was surprised when he laughed. It was mean. "I'm buying that little flat cornfield between them two, today. The Richmans think they's better than me, but they'll come off their high horse when I wave that deed in front of their faces!"

I remembered what my stepfather had said when he agreed to my marrying the old man. "I don't know why Old Man Hershall stayed in Nelson County after his wife died and his son Big Jakie moved back here to the hills with the other Hershalls and Fieldings. Unless he means to buy out the Catholics an acre or two at a time."

The spring weather was undecided. Sometimes a fast-moving squall would pass over, and sometimes it would come a heavy downpour. Gray skies made everything hazy and the air still had plenty of bite, yet the new leaves in the treetops swayed real gentle like. Warm weather had come in enough for the redbud trees to bloom, then it had turned off cold again. A light snow laid in circles around the bases of the trees and along fencerows. But it would melt fast and Redbud Winter would be over. Along the roadside, trumpet-shaped bluebells nodded.

Nothing excepting the bottomlands looked like it made for good farming since it was mostly rocks on hillsides. You couldn't call them mountains, for they were nowhere near as tall as what I saw where I grew up. Although, I did think Landing Run made a picture book — giant pines and cedars crowding along the gentle swelling ridges, and bare branches of pin oaks, red maples and elms reaching straight up toward the sky. And in the middle of the gently rolling fields and woodland, a creek laughing and bubbling along.

Landing Run Creek was handy for families getting water to their houses and barns, and though Mr. Hershall spoke little of it, I knew he got his money operating a whiskey-making still. His daddy, Notice Hershall, Sr., had built it back in the woods in 1824, beside one of them rushing springs that feeds into the creek. Nobody felt moonshining was anything wrong, just not legal if you didn't pay taxes on it. Which cost half the price.

A lot of the men who paid my husband for whiskey earned their wages by working at John L. Meadors' sawmill. It was built over a deep place in the water that runs close to the Beech Fork that empties into the Rolling Fork of the Salt River.

I speculated if any other men worked a shine. I see a lot of them skirting our house to slip into the trees and out again in a few minutes. I imagine they carry a bottle or a jar tucked inside their shirts. The Catholics say it is a sin to get drunk, but they sure don't mind a person drinking.

Mr. Hershall set the horse into an easy four-beat gait aiming to put us in Bardstown a little short of an hour's time. All the way, we passed by an uneven rise and fall in the rolling hills with higher knobs in the background.

When we crossed the covered bridge over the Beech Fork River, I looked into the pretty water and pictured how many people had traveled it since the white men had settled here in the late 1700s. The sycamores' white bark showed up stark against the brown of the other trees and matted underbrush.

As we reached the main street in Bardstown, I saw men dressed in overalls and baggy suit coats with wool toboggans pulled over their ears. They rode horses and drove wagons and hitched up along the concrete sidewalks aiming to trade at the hardware store and the buggy shop. Quite a few gentlemen were dressed in fine suit coats and felt hats. One kicked his muddy overshoes against the cut stone edging of the walkway before going into the bank at the corner. The saloons and pool halls were on the other side of the street.

Mr. Hershall pulled the buggy up to a hitching rail around Courthouse Square set in the middle of four streets. The court building was fancy, made of stone and red brick with wood framing. It had more than one roof—all steep-sloped and decorated on top with little circle towers with pointed roofs and rows of curlicue stone brackets jutting out from the roof overhang. There was semi-circle arches on the windows and steps leading to a big arch doorway in front.

The first women I saw was in a buggy stopped not too far from us. It was Annie Richman and Bertie Linkahan.

Mr. Hershall named them to me, with a sneer. "Them Catlick women have eight and nine kids apiece so's they can keep outnumbering ever body else!"

Gathering up her cloak and full skirts and petticoats, Miz Annie stood up in the buggy. She looked about my mother's age, tall and big around the middle. She couldn't see very well, for she studied the buggy wheel, looking up and down real careful. Her husband, Garr Richman, rubbed one arm while he got out the driver side to help her. He leaned on a cane.

Bertie heaved herself out of the buggy on her own, a hefty woman with round red cheeks. She turned and walked toward the stores on the east side.

Miz Annie stopped still when she peered over at our buggy. I smiled, but she was already looking away. I didn't know whether she saw me or not but it seemed like she was mad at me and I didn't even know her.

"Pull them kivvers over you and the boy," Mr. Hershall said. "The wind's getting up." He rushed inside the courthouse and Miz Annie and her husband walked right beside our buggy. When she passed me, I couldn't quit looking at her. I nodded my head and smiled again, but just a little. I didn't want to look like I was gloating, for Mr. Hershall was waiting to sign the deed to take over the Richmans' cornfield.

I jumped out of the buggy, opened the great latch on the iron-studded courthouse door, and held it open for Miz Annie and Mr. Richman.

"Why, thank you, Emmalene. That's right nice of you." Annie knew my name! Her kind voice made me want to cry for something but I didn't know what.

I put Jakie far back into the buggy and tucked lap robes around him. Then I sat in the driver's seat behind the horse. The courthouse being in the middle of everything gave me a clear view of downtown. I counted eleven buildings with tall windows. Most had awnings above the doorways.

A shopkeeper dressed in a white shirt and dark vest stood in front of his place of business and I made out the name on the sign, "Spalding's Dry Goods Store." He probably sold fancy dresses and powder sachets along with work boots and handkerchiefs. I decided I would come back later by myself and get a good look inside that store.

A horse and wagon stopped at the hitching rail in the empty space beside our buggy. The driver caught my eye, and he smiled real big. His face was dark and his mouth was heavy with teeth. He wore an ill-fitting suit and his trousers fit tight against his big legs. Something in the way he looked me over caused me to turn away, but I liked it just the same.

"You're Emmalene Hershall," he said. "Kind of a cold day for April ain't it?"

I nodded and thought what to answer, but the man spoke up again. "My name's Albert Nobles and I live back Landing Run Road a little past you all."

"Glad to meet you," I said, not knowing what else to say. Mr. Hershall had told me that Albert and his wife and kids was the closest neighbors on our side of the road and owned a apple orchard.

"Well, I got to get these apples on down to the grocery store," he said. "I dug them up this morning where they been buried all winter."

I watched him turn around to a peck basket in the back of his wagon. The buttons on his jacket strained across his chest as he rummaged in the straw and pulled out two red apples.

"Don't look like they just come off the tree but they're not bad. Here," he said, and handed me two apples.

"One's for the boy." Albert looked pleased with himself.

"Thanks," I said and watched him pick up the reins in his big hands.

As he drove off, he looked back at me and his smile changed into a frown. I looked behind me and saw Bertie Linkahan standing in Spalding's doorway staring at us.

Bertie wore a coat that covered her dress down to her shoes and had a round flat hat sitting on top of mounds of hair, stacked up and pulled back. The smirk on her face told me she had seen enough to tell Annie Richman and all her women friends that I was flirting with a married man and would be after their husbands and sons.

I never thought I was flirting, but later on when I first saw Dolin, and him being such a good-looking, red-headed young man, I had to allow Bertie would not want me any wheres near her son.

Les
April 1910

$\mathcal{At}$ twelve years old, my friend Dolin Linkahan and me didn't need no more schooling. We already could read, do cursive and figure numbers, so at least we wouldn't get cheated when we sold a bale of hay or dreamed about being the first in Landing Run to buy a new 1910 Model T machine to drive instead of a horse and buggy. So we quit school and went to working at John L. Meadors' sawmill.

Dolin stands half a head taller than me and is a little meatier. His easy speeches and red hair gets girls to grinning when he's around, whereas I mostly keep my mouth closed so tight it looks like I don't have any lips. Dolin said, "Les, you got a good face, not too pretty, but smart-looking." That made me laugh. "But you got to say something so's they'll notice you."

For some reason, John L.'s daughter, Maribelle, noticed me over the other men who worked at her daddy's sawmill. Maybe because I didn't flirt with her and go on about her looks. Or maybe because I was Christina and Nan Mary's half-brother and those girls all hung around each other and talked about boys.

She favored me, a man of twenty, and asked me over on Sundays. Before long, she said we was courting, while Dolin talked about Old Man Hershall's new young wife.

"Emmalene's got a face sweeter than a angel, til you get to her eyes," he said. "Them eyes look like they know a secret, and her mouth turns up like it's a funny secret."

I first saw Emmalene up close when Dr. Beale in his buggy and I on my horse both met her in the road between two turnoffs—one, the Linkahans, and next to it our Richman lane. Opposite was the road back to Old Man Hershall's farm.

Emmalene stopped walking and let her shawl loose from her

head, and I saw her hair was dark and curly and way past her shoulders.

The doctor smiled real big and took off his hat. "Hello, young lady, I'm Dr. Franklin Beale, and you must be the new Mrs. Hershall."

"Call me Emmalene," she said, looking at me. I nodded and mumbled, "How'd do."

"This quiet fellow is Les Richman," Dr. Beale said with a wink. "Les isn't bashful, he's just not given to much talk."

Emmalene smiled, first at me, then at the doctor.

"Can I give you a ride?" Doctor Beale said. "It's no trouble."

I couldn't help staring, for when Emmalene shaded her eyes, her shawl fell away and showed her full woman's figure. I turned my head so she wouldn't see me looking so hard. I didn't mean to disrespect her but her eyes pierced my face like she was climbing inside me. I wanted to turn my horse and barrel away, and stay at the same time.

"No, thanks, Doctor. I'm only going back to the house," she said, covering her hair again. She turned down the Hershall lane.

I coughed and shifted in my saddle. Dr. Beale laughed at me and clucked to his horse.

"Look out there, Les," he said. "She's married, even if her old husband sleeps out there beside his moonshine."

Old Man Hershall and Emmalene wasn't Catholic—Papa and I neither. But most everybody in Landing Run was one or else married one. That's how I got raised up with a houseful of them. My own mother died when I was a boy, then Papa married Maw, who was a Catholic and they had eight more kids.

Catholics don't think making whiskey and drinking is a sin, but smearing around another man's wife is. I thought neither Dolin nor me ought to be favoring Emmalene.

Emmalene
May 1910

Sometimes I think about ways I could've stopped what happened. It was May 18, the day of Halley's Comet, and lots of folks was getting together at Rice's Store. Miz Rice got the newspapers and had read everything about the comet. She said she was having a party when its tail come through its brightest. "Some thinks it'll collide with the world and kill us all, but Pope Pius the Tenth said it was all overblown stories. I'm with the pope," she said.

Mr. Hershall had took Jakie with him to the shack in the woods and, like every time I got lonesome, I set out walking to the store.

Same as Miz Rice, I wasn't scared of the comet. I packed up my eggs on top of a covered dish of fried chicken and biscuits and lit out.

As I got to Landing Run Road, Albert Nobles brought up his farm wagon beside me.

Usually, I turned down his offer of a ride, but Albert acted like it was a favor to him. "Hey, Emmalene," he said, "can I buy a dozen eggs off you before you carry them to Rice's? That way you won't have to give them a cut of your money."

I do love a bargain, but I should have said no. My fast-beating heart could have told me the truth, but a powerful need for somebody to notice me and regard me with favor drove clear thought out of my head. The right day, the right minute had come and I found myself climbing up to the seat beside him.

While I settled my basket and smoothed my skirts, I caught him staring at me. He glanced away, then looked back again. I felt my face flush with my heart pumping so fast. I stole looks at him too, guessing him to be about thirty and a very healthy man. His legs were great logs, not shriveled and bowed like the shape left in Mr. Hershall's dirty overalls.

"Ain't it a pretty day?" Albert said.

I told myself that talking about the weather to a married man was okay, but Albert got personal real quick. "How do you like your house?" he asked.

Before I could say, he had another question. "How do you like being married to the old man?" He didn't wait for that answer either. When he started talking, the words came fast, and he didn't stop. I saw that he had no one to talk to, either.

"Nora just won't say nothing to me," Albert said about his wife. "She talks to the kids, spoils them to death, but she won't even look me in the face and say two words."

Something about his sadness touched me, but swift-like he changed his tone and praised my rose-colored dress. "That color suits you just like red on a apple."

I puzzled how he come up with such a thing, but I'd been hoping he'd say something like that.

When we got to the Boone's pig farm, Albert turned the wagon opposite their driveway and onto the dirt trail with weeds dead from winter pushed to the sides. I'd heard it led to the Boone's tenant house. I should have told him to keep on Landing Run Road and get on to the Rices' celebration. But I said nothing.

Albert said, "I know where you can get a cold, good drink of water."

He pulled the wagon up to the two-room cabin and I left my heavy basket on the seat while we went inside.

I could hear water splashing in the next room. We walked past a straw pallet in front of the empty fireplace and into the little kitchen. From a spring that fed into the creek, water flowed without stopping through a pipe to the tin sink. It splattered against the bottom, and circled down the drain.

I stood there with Albert big and warm behind me. I thought I saw a movement at the back window but when I walked over, there was nothing but a glade, a small clearing dipping into the woods.

I come to my senses. "Get me out of here!"

Albert had to talk me into letting him at least drive me in the wagon to Landing Run Road.

I had come to Landing Run as the outsider, and two months later this mistake—almost nothing—got told around. It looked like the coming of Halley's Comet was bringing awful bad luck for me. As I recollected, my misfortunes started even before I left the mountains. For Jarboe had told me the last time we was wandering the mountainside where we grew up, "She's short and she's fat and she jibber-jabbers all time, but I love her. And I can't deny her and my first-coming baby."

So I hid out by coming to Landing Run, and now that would be spoiled too.

My leanings toward Albert Nobles changed in a instant. I went from craving his attention like a dry rose soaks up warm rain, to disgust with him and myself in causing more gossip. It looked like I would never belong, anywhere.

Les
May 1910

They said Halley's Comet would come closest to the earth on May 18, and it was an exciting thing in Landing Run. Old-timers claimed it was a bad sign, and I heard tell some men drank and some was on their knees praying and fearing it was the end times. I thought it sure was opposite ways of facing the truth, but most people looked for it to be something wondrous, a bigger light coming after what had been growing in the sky for a week or more.

Miz Rice out to the store was having a picnic that started in the afternoon and a moonlight dance when it got dark. They already had a wood platform built to hold the dancers off the ground and a place for the fiddler and caller to stand. I didn't aim to go, for I wanted to sit by myself and think. I told Maribelle that my sisters were going. "You go on with Christina and Nan Mary and them."

She wasn't very happy about that and pouted. "Well, are we courting or not? If you were really my beau, looks like you'd want to take me to sit with and eat our supper and dance with me while the comet passes."

I didn't want to argue, so I just tipped my hat and got on my horse and turned him back toward home. I knowed she was right. But I just couldn't think of getting ever body in the notion that I was going to marry her. I recollected that when I used to eat Sunday dinner over at Meadors' house, Retta would open up the front parlor for me and Maribelle to set. But nobody could get me on that couch inside talking about the weather or anything else. I would set on the porch swing with her but long about sunset I was always ready to leave and go feed the stock and get in firewood for Maw Richman.

My horse must have thought about riding through the cornfield before I did, for I don't remember how we got there. The meadow in the bottom lands didn't belong to Richmans anymore and I had give up on an idea that someday I might build me a log house in that valley when I started housekeeping with a woman and having kids.

It wasn't right for me to be there, for Old Man Hershall had bought the property off Maw over a month ago and he felt pretty strong about what all was his. I knowed it broke Maw's tender heart to sell it, for it'd belonged to her Greenhaven family ever since they settled in Nelson County. Seemed like ever body loved this little piece of ground.

I rode the length of the lot til I got to the woods and the hedge of Osage orange trees. They didn't grow any fruit to eat, but I remembered how Dolin and me used to play fort, and throw the warty balls at each other. I guided my horse under the thorny arch where the branches spread out and locked their tops together. My horse stopped to munch on one of last year's green hedge apples, but I turned him onto the path in the woods between the two knobs where Linkahans lived on one and we lived on the other. Voices traveled good when a body on either hill would halloo across and tell the other some piece of news or get the other to come over and visit.

It was still a little daylight, so Halley's Comet didn't show up much in the sky yet. I backtracked my horse down to where Landing Run Road and the creek runs together. My favorite resting place was thick with trees, and the wild currant bushes made the air smell like cloves. The creek was trickling over little rocks standing up in its bed and the sound was a comfort to me. I could see who all passed on the road, but they couldn't see me.

First person I beheld was Emmalene. I couldn't take my eyes off her. Her arms was covered with her shawl, but I remembered what they looked like the day I first saw her up close—all round and soft and needing hugging.

She carried a big split-oak basket covered over with a tea towel and I pondered who would sit with her at the Rice's picnic supper dance and if she made a pie like most of the women. Jakie wasn't along, so I figured he was in the woods with his Grandpaw.

I wasn't free to think about Emmalene. She being married legal, if not in body, was one thing, but Dolin had his eyes on her too. He mooned over her black curls and white arms and said how he heard her laugh one day. "It's like water tinkling over ice chunks in a glass," he said. And him being my best pal, I couldn't tell him I felt more than he did. For I had met her up close, too, and seen her dimples and how she looked deep in my eyes and how I felt a spell was put on me. I had to listen to him say he wished she'd leave Old Man Hershall and then he'd have a chance with her. And I couldn't say how I wished the same thing for me.

Emmalene was still in sight, walking along the road when Albert Nobles pulled his wagon up beside her. I watched him lean down and say something and I saw her climb up onto the wagon seat. I thought one thing, then another. She didn't need a ride—all able-bodied people walked out the three miles to Rice's Store and never thought nothing about it. Kids walked it ever day during school term. And Emmalene herself walked once a week or so as she had eggs to sell.

But she had that heavy basket and maybe it was weighing her down. I was giving her ever kind of excuse to ride with Albert, who is a philandering man and ever body knows it. Just because his wife packs up and goes to her mother's ever time one of the kids sneezes, don't mean he can act single.

I sat there brooding for pretty near twenty minutes. Then I saw Emmalene hurrying back like as if the basket was empty, but it didn't swing much so I knowed it was still heavy. She didn't turn into the Hershall lane, but went into the woods across the creek from me. I could just make out the outline of her sitting down on the ledge of rock on their property.

I heard her crying and I wanted to get up and find Albert Nobles and punch in his face, for I knowed it was him caused it.

After a while, she got quiet and I figgered she didn't see me, hid like I was. Somehow or nother, it pleasured me to know I was on one side, her on the other—both of us alone with each other.

When the dark sky began to show up the comet and its tail, I commenced to hope she knew I was there, and I pretended we were looking at the sky together. It was a ball of light, four times bigger than the brightest star I could see, yet a lot smaller than the moon, with a fuzzy streak of tail. It put me in the mind of a giant match head just struck and got flung away and flamed up the wooden part. And the flaming part was like hair streaming out.

I could of stayed all night sitting in my hiding place even though it was lit up in the light of the comet, but when Emmalene stood up and walked back toward the Hershall farmhouse, I thought I'd better get my horse to the barn and take care of him.

That new spring night with the frogs croaking by the creek and a old hooty owl somewhere in the woods made me feel closer to Emmalene than I'd ever known with another human. I also felt like a fool, for she probably didn't even know I was there. It was kind of like the whole thing was in my mind. But—real or not—the night of the comet was a pretty good dream to store up inside my head and live out again whenever I got lonesome.

Emmalene
June 1910

It was the beginning of summer and the only neighbors I saw was the Rices. It was already hot weather and I liked to take Jakie down to our Hershall side of the creek where the trees grow thick and the birds sing the loudest. Standing in a certain spot I could see the bottomland that Mr. Hershall had bought off the Richmans. They had needed the money to save their home from being sold, but the old man said they hated him all the more for his owning the best part of their land.

"I ain't planting nary crop or using it," he said. "Just letting it set there as a token that I'm ever bit the worth of them, Catholic or no."

By rights, I could have gone to the cornfield, but I didn't. It was a pink-sky evening, and Jakie and I sat in the scrub grass and loam of rotted stumps and listened to the fiddle. It was Garr playing "Goodbye Liza Jane" and we could hear the buzz of all the goings-on of the Richmans and Linkahans across the creek.

I kept my voice low so's no one would find our hiding place. "Jakie, don't you lean out too far or you'll fall headfirst into the water."

Jakie stood on a rock that hung over the bank, poking the weeds and briars with a stick, barely moving them with a light sweep.

The fiddle and guitar music floated over me, but hearing the two families talking together made me ache. Mostly what I heard from my husband was, "What'd the boy eat today?" or "Did you get the cow milked before dark?"

Sometimes I thought maybe Mr. Hershall wanted to talk a little and used Jakie as a way to start. But other times, it seemed he scorned me and wished I would leave.

Jakie pointed all five fingers at the water striders landing on the moss-covered stones. He giggled every time a toad frog splashed the water.

Of a sudden, he reached out, his foot slipped and he fell from the bank, legs and arms flying. He didn't scream. His shirt caught on the twisted limbs of a tree which held him, feet dangling.

"Oh, my Lord! Jakie!" I yelled, and pushed back branches. I got my skirt tangled in a grape vine that curled down from a tree limb.

Before I could reach Jakie, I heard something crashing through the thicket. I saw a young man push branches and vines to the side and reach for Jakie.

It was Dolin Linkahan. "You're okay, Son. I got you."

Jakie never made a sound, just melted into Dolin's arms.

I took the boy's small, white hand. "Are you hurt? Did you scrape yourself?" Jakie looked so calm, it made me think. What does he know about danger?

When I looked in Dolin's face, his attention washed over me.

I dropped to my knees, shaking all over. "I thought he was going into the water," I said. Then my body went limp and I folded my arms around myself.

"He's all right," Dolin said, "but I think he scared you half to death."

Dolin took my arm and helped me stand. I'd never seen him up close and he was taller than I thought. His hair was reddish, like sorghum molasses.

"I wish I had you a drink of whiskey," he said. "That would stop your nerves."

As we walked back to the farmhouse, Dolin guided Jakie with one hand, and held branches out of our way with the other. He seemed to listen for every step I took. I let myself get lost in the feeling of having a friend and wished I could hold the spell forever.

Les
July 1910

Maribelle had grown up seeing me at the sawmill, but one night she surprised me.

"I don't like you working over there."

"Not work for your own daddy?" I didn't know if I had heard her right.

"One time a man got his leg cut deep, and I have nightmares thinking it will happen to you," she said. She lowered her eyes, picking at the ribbons on her bodice. "And besides, I don't like it when your ears ring long after quitting time, and you get splinters in your hands."

Which seemed to be my misfortune, not hers. I clenched my jaw. "We are not married, and even if we were, you'd not be telling me what to do or not to!"

Maribelle ran into the house, maybe crying. She liked to put on a show and I never really knew if her feelings was hurt.

Maw Richman didn't boss me, but she was scared for me too—working in that hot place with dangerous blades. She was fond of John L.—him being her sister's husband—yet she thought he was running us too hard. "Les, you and Dolin and all the others have worked like dogs all through this July heat!"

I didn't mind the work. Whether it was cutting down trees around the county, or planing them to a exact thickness—it paid good money. I could make close to a dollar a day, and the heat, dust and god-awful noise toughened me up, kept me skinny but strong. Also, I liked the men I worked with. John L. said they did better for me than him.

I could have left Landing Run and got a job anyplace, but I stayed at Meadors Sawmill. Maybe I'd marry little Maribelle, but the main reason was I couldn't leave Maw and Papa with looking after all the kids. His inflamed rheumatiz had got so bad he couldn't work, not even in the garden.

Truth was, I didn't want to leave. Maw treated me as good as her own and I loved the rolling hills of Kentucky, back away from most people. Just those we knew all our lives.

Papa wasn't any religion, and I wasn't forced either, though Maw would have given a lot to see us baptized. John L. was Catholic—that's why he let us off one day a week. Against his religion to work on Sunday.

On one such Sunday afternoon when I was sitting in the porch swing with Maribelle, John L. said, "Come on and ride over with me." He couldn't stay away from his mill, not even for one day.

When the saw was quiet, it didn't seem like the same place. It was real nice with just a riffle of wind carrying the smell of Queen Anne's lace and fescue grass.

John L. stood with his hands behind his back and talked about taking his part in the big timber boom in Kentucky. "Yessir," he said. "We do it all—drag a tree from the woods, put it through the sawmill and haul it to the railroad siding. We're doing right good."

I nodded and listened. Somewhere in the woods was something dead—maybe a coon or a squirrel—the stink mixed in with the sweet smell of hay.

John L. rocked back and forth. "I got another pricey job from a Bardstown construction company, starting tomorrow." His eyes glowed. "Tell your Maw you won't be home at dinnertime. And don't look for you home at supper, neither."

The sun blared scorching hot on our flat workplace. A wood roof offered some shade, yet we sweated through our clothes and my socks were even wet. We drank from the water bucket the boys brought round, then slung some of the cold water from the dipper over our heads and shoulders.

The saw-box, built right over Landing Run Creek, had free-running water coming through an inch-wide pipe to the boiler. When the engine got fired up with a good head of steam, it had power to pull the blade—that's what done the sawing. Over and over, the saw whined from a high pitch noise down to a moan as it dragged its turning blade into the hard wood.

Sam Greenhaven was the one stoking the firebox. Many's the time I'd heard him brag, "I'm gonna fire that engine up to hell and back!" He kept filling the wood box til the smoke rolled out of the smokestack.

One man handed Dolin a log; they fed the blade while I pulled the pieces from the end of the saw carriage. When I turned to hand off to the man beyond me, I heard something sounded like dynamite—it shook the whole sawmill.

Next thing I knew, I hit the ground thirty feet away, my wind knocked out.

I laid there not knowing who I was for a while. My ears rung like a bell, but all else was quiet. No wood thrush or meadowlark singing in the trees along the creek, no cicadas buzzing in the hot grass.

Then I heard the dinner gong, clanging, clanging. It didn't sound like good things, like us bringing out lunch buckets of fried meat and biscuits. It sounded evil.

My whole body hurt, and my shirt was tore to pieces. I looked around at the men, some of them staggering to their feet, some laying there crying out. I saw John L., his face white and hard while he ran around shouting from one man to another, "Are you hurt?—Are you okay?"

He came up to me, and took a deep breath. "Oh, thank God, Les, you're all right."

Looking around, he yelled, "Where's Dolin?"

He grabbed my arm to help me up and must have seen my face. "Sorry," he said.

We saw Dolin at the same time. He laid on the ground, away from us. He wasn't moving.

It took me longer to get to him, hobbling like I was. John L. knelt close to Dolin. "He's still breathing."

The left side of Dolin's face was blood red and his britches was all tore. His eyes was closed, and I worried if he got hit by a piece of metal or a log or what.

John L. yelled, "Some of you all go get Dr. Beale. Take my horse… hurry!"

Instead of going home, I went with the men carrying Dolin to his mother's house.

With him being out, they put white sheets over a farm slide and hand-carried him so not to jostle so much.

It wasn't no time til Dr. Beale got to Bertie's.

Emmalene
July 1910

Rice's Store served as a trading house for cabins and log homes strung together in the woods and knobs back off the road along Landing Run Creek. Some women brought in eggs like I did. Some brought live chickens in a wire pen. Annie Richman had one of her kids bring her churned butter to trade and a seamstress had a pink-checked dress for sale. It was full of buttons and rick-rack and hung in the window where the sun brightened it. The homegrown and homemade things were traded for what folks couldn't grow or make for ourselves, like coffee, sugar, coal oil, matches and such.

The day everything changed in Landing Run was in hottest July. Miz Rice had said to me, "You've brought in enough eggs to trade for six yards of goods." I stood at the end of a counter in the store picking out a blue and white flowerdy print to make a new housedress.

I asked myself if Jarboe Clemons, or my step-father, Ernest Fielding, and his sons, Hack and Conrad, back in Clay County ever remembered Emmalene Hershall, married to the man with the most money in Landing Run—and me making my own money, too.

Of a sudden, a loud explosion came from the direction of Landing Run Creek, enough that the store windows rattled their glass panes. My first thought was somebody was attacking me. I wouldn't be surprised. Yet, usually, no one paid me any mind.

Everybody knew at the same time that it was something awful happened back in Landing Run. People forgot they were avoiding me while we all scrambled out the door.

"The sawmill's blowed up!" yelled a man and he ran toward his horse.

I let out my breath when I realized it was a business concern and not anybody's house. I left my tote bag and egg basket and jumped in the wagon with Mr. Rice. The whole store emptied with everybody racing toward the explosion.

A rider coming from the sawmill said, "They's bringing a injured man to Bertie Linkahan's place, and somebody has rode back out to Jackson Highway to get Dr. Beale!"

Those on horseback passed us, but we were among the first ones to reach the lane to Bertie's house. Along the way, people was shouting, "What happened?—Is anybody killed?" It was almost like a picnic even though it surely was something terrible going on.

My neighbors described what they were doing when they heard the blast. "I was scalding tomatoes..." said a woman in a red-stained apron, while a man in dusty overalls yelled to anyone listening, "I was throwing hay down to the mule. The noise just about blasted me out of the hayloft..."

For the first time, people looked at me while they talked, forgot who I was—the outsider, the bad girl.

I held my skirt with both hands and walked up the incline of Bertie's back yard with the rest. Everyone had rushed to get there but then milled around not knowing whether to knock. A couple of ladies from the Women's Sodality of Our Lady of Hope Church entered the screen door, but the men stood smoking in the yard, wandering around talking about the accident.

Dr. Beale drove up in his buggy and threw his reins to a barefoot boy. After the kid tied up the horse to the fence post, he strutted, shoulders back. "Dr. Beale said he hopes who ever they saved is not bad burned."

My stomach knotted when I heard who it was—Bertie's son, Dolin. Sweat broke out on my face and under my arms. I dreaded to know what had happened, yet I pulled on the young boy's sleeve, "What about Dolin? How bad off is he?"

"He's not come to yet is what somebody said who was there," a man told me.

All was in a uproar at Bertie's including her bunch of young boys running and shouting. I thought they was covering up the fear of their oldest brother being hurt.

It was mostly women in the kitchen while Dr. Beale looked at Dolin in the room where Bertie's bed was.

Dr. Beale came out and washed his hands saying, "That young man needs constant care. His burns are minor, but he's in and out of consciousness and needs a quiet place to rest and get well. Away from all the noise here."

I found myself almost pleading to help.

"Bring him over to my house. It's peaceful there and airish with the breeze coming in the windows—and I can look after him." My voice sounded giddy even in my own ears.

Dr. Beale coughed. "Will Mr. Hershall be all right with us bringing Dolin over?"

"He stays mostly at the…in back of the farm," I said, catching myself.

Already, I was thinking what I would tell the old man. I would say that Bertie was paying us fifty cents a day to take care of Dolin. I would take my egg money and give it to Mr. Hershall in advance. That would keep him from complaining. Little Jakie, in his gentle way wouldn't make any noise. I could help Dolin where no one else could.

Dr. Beale opened his eyes wide at me. "Well, that would be perfect. Where his skin is burned needs bandages but they're not serious. I got other calls I have to make, so he needs you to be there to make sure he comes around, to watch him, through tonight."

Bertie Linkahan pressed her lips tight. "Well now, Doctor, why are you figgering to move Dolin away from his own home and his mother to care for him?"

"Bertie, listen. You want that boy to get plenty of rest."

Bertie bent over Dolin, smoothing his hair and telling him something although maybe he couldn't hear. The womenfolk stood around watching in sorrow for the grieving mother.

Annie bent down to hear my whisper.

"Do you think Miz Bertie won't let me take care of Dolin? I know what she thinks…" I stopped, and then began again, "I know she don't favor me."

It was Bertie that had told ever body that she saw me, a married woman, flirting with Albert who is also married. Naturally, she would think I was a trifling woman and going after her son.

Les
July 1910

The morning after the sawmill blast, I woke up awful sore from being throwed around. I didn't have a job to go to, so come daylight I rode over to the Hershall's. Dr. Beale was leaving Emmalene's when he saw me. He had stopped by first thing to see if Dolin was any better.

"Les, that young woman is not just a pretty girl. She's an impressive nurse." He pulled a cigar from the inside pocket of his suit coat.

He offered me one but I shook my head. "Is Dolin woke up?" I said, my belly in a knot.

"Yes, Emmalene said he came to for awhile and was in pain. She was afraid to give him the laudanum I left because it would knock him back out. But she props him up and gives him willow bark tea." The doctor ran a finger around the edge of his high-standing shirt collar, wilted of all its starch.

"Has he said anything?"

"He has not come fully awake enough to talk, so I can't tell the whole extent of his injuries. I'm coming back to see him tonight and every day til I know what we're dealing with. I know one thing—Emmalene is taking the best possible care of him. He couldn't do better."

When I climbed the wooden steps and knocked on Emmalene's door, I expected she'd look tired, but she swung open the door, her face beaming. Did the red roses in her dress made her face so pink?

"Come on in, Les."

"How is he?" I said, holding my hat.

"He's probably still asleep." She turned the glass doorknob to the sickroom as delicate as if it was a egg. The door creaked anyway.

"He opens his eyes and then drops off again," said Emmalene.

"Dr. Beale feels pretty sure he doesn't have a bad head wound, but we don't know yet."

I walked close to the bed. Dolin wore a sleeveless undershirt and homemade side-tie drawers. The skin on the left side of his face was red and puffy and he was missing some eyebrows and eyelashes. He breathed heavy with his mouth open.

Emmalene changed Dolin's dressings while I watched. When she took off the bloody gauze, I sucked in my breath. He was going to have a big scar under his eye and down his cheek.

I watched her lay wet gauze, rinsed out in cool water and carbolic acid, on the raw wound. Dolin moaned but didn't open his eyes. She laid a clean sheet over him, real gentle like.

At the kitchen table, me and her drank coffee. She told me she also lost her mother when she was young. She had left her stepfather, Ernest Fielding, and two stepbrothers in the mountains when the old man offered her a chance to have her own home in Landing Run, without the usual man-and-woman kind of marriage.

With Emmalene's not being a Catholic, we had something else between us. I guess that's why it wasn't hard to talk to her. "What did the old man have to say about Dolin being here?" I asked.

"He spends most ever night in the woods. He doesn't care about me taking care of him."

"What about you giving up your room? Have you got a place to sleep?" I didn't look at her, just rubbed the side of my nose.

"I made myself a pallet outside the door. I'm okay."

Emmalene changed the subject. "I hear that you and Maribelle are talking to each other."

I set my cup down. "Well, I'm not so sure how that's going. Since the sawmill blew yesterday, I'm out of work."

I decided to ask Emmalene's opinion about working for her husband. "Do you reckon he could use a paid hand?"

"I don't rightly know any of Mr. Hershall's business. Why don't you go on back to the woods and ask him?"

Along with other men around here, I'd not been in Old Man Hershall's house until Dolin got hurt, but I knew that behind his farmyard and cornfield there was a certain bend in an old white sycamore tree, and the sound of rushing limestone water over a fall of jutting rocks. I pushed through the scrub brush and the tangle of grapevines hanging in the tops of water oaks until I stood behind a clump of saplings.

I spotted Mr. Hershall sitting on a stack of logs. Under a squashed, dirty hat, his hair showed white and his shoulders were stooped, but I could see there was still strength enough in his body.

The old man had scooped out a shallow flat-bottomed trench and built a fire, which burned low under a rack on legs, a make-do stove. My stomach growled at the smell of fried rabbit and gravy in a uncovered skillet. A shotgun lay propped against the logs beside him, its steel barrel flashing in the sun.

I cupped my hands around my mouth and gave three calls of the turtledove. Sometimes we did that as a warning and Mr. Hershall, with his head and upper body still bent forward, grabbed his gun. He didn't take aim, just turned his ear toward my call and then I saw he recognized me.

He motioned me into camp and offered me a tin cup of coffee and a plate of rabbit stew. I had not seen him for a while, but he looked the same with white hair, yet his eyebrows and patches of beard were still red-tinged. Because of his fierce looks and ways, strangers was taken aback to hear him talk, for his voice scratched out with a high-tone pitch, like a real old lady.

"What you doing over here this time of morning?"

We sat talking friendly for a good bit and I thought to say, "You and Emmalene's doing a good thing by taking in Dolin like this."

The old man squeaked, "Yeah, she said something about it. I don't care what she does as long as she takes care of the boy."

I finished my meal, rolled a cigarette and lit it with a burning twig. The old man chewed his tobacco, spitting small streams into the fire, causing it to hiss. I could smell the sweetness of his chew, which he made himself by dampening the dried leaves with maple syrup before twisting it.

"Reckon you heard when the sawmill blowed," I said.

"Heard it?" the old man giggled in his high voice. "I seen it! A board come flying over the trees by the creek and landed yonder in that there clump of pines. Must have blew a good three mile." He pointed where the creek runs into the river at the spot he guessed the sawmill had been.

"You don't say." I grinned and shook my head. It sounded like a tall tale, but it made a good story.

My back itched in the sun. "Don't reckon the law comes back here," I said.

"Not lately, anyways. I keep everything quiet and to myself—don't strut my onions."

I got down to my business. "Would you be needing a paid hand here on the shine?"

The old man thought on it a while. Country people have a way of not speaking until they know what they've got to say.

I was thinking too. The old man don't like Catholics but I ain't one. And anyway he trusts them enough to buy his whiskey and keep shut about where they got it.

"Summertime ain't the best season—ever how, it's still a heap of work needs doing," Mr. Hershall finally said. "Understand, I don't take on partners and I pay in whiskey—no cash. If that'd suit you, then I'd be proud to hire you on."

"It's a fair enough deal," I said. "As long as you know I'm not bound to shoot for another man's still."

We locked eyes and that made a contract better than a signing or a handshake.

"All right. All right," said the old man, smiling and nodding his head.

"When do you care for me to start?"

"Early tomorrow morning is as good a time as any."

Leading my horse out of the woods toward home, I took pleasure imagining a job close to Emmalene, yet common sense nagged at me. How could my heart thump at the thought of her—not only the old man's wife, but also my best friend's dream girl? When Dolin woke up, he would fall more in love for sure. And was I or wasn't I courting Maribelle? Why did she come up short when put up side Emmalene?

I got on my horse at Landing Run Road and spied John L.'s buggy.

"Hey there, Les. Just the man I'd hope to see."

I followed John L. to where his sawmill used to be, its splintered housing still straddling the deepest bend in the creek. From the higher bank, water poured through a ragged edge of pipe. Metal fragments of sharp tinplate glinted in the sun and a few stray logs, splintered and broken, lay scattered in the yard.

I stared at the packed earth of wood shavings where I had worked beside Dolin yesterday when both our lives had changed. I pictured his red eyebrows dusted white with sawdust, could see the sweat caked into the laugh wrinkles around his eyes.

John L. and I stood smelling honeysuckle along with bitter weeds and stinkbugs. He said, "I'm fixing to rebuild and I'd like you to oversee it, plus the running of the mill, afterward."

A rake-handled tool was propped against the sagging shed. Someone had removed its hinged hook making it useless. A tin dinner pail hung on a big nail beside it.

"I have to think on it," I said.

John L. pulled his eyebrows together, but he didn't push me. "Just let me know. Just let me know."

Going home, I rode my horse slow. First no job, now two. I knew sawmilling, knew how to treat workers right; but I was troubled over

John L.'s offer.

How long has he been planning this? Does he know that me and Maribelle are barely speaking? What if the whole thing is her idea? I could picture her pouting and begging her daddy to give me a manager's job. Making me a foreman would suit Maribelle—about as much as she wouldn't like me moonshining.

Dread tugged at me—not going to work in Mr. Hershall's shine would mean losing Emmalene's company. I forced myself to push back the picture of her face, eyes full of spirit and smile full welcome.

The next morning I had no doubt which place I was going to work. I don't know if my knees tightened against the saddle or if my fingers twitched on the reins, but my horse headed straight toward the Hershall lane, and I knew he was happy with my decision.

Emmalene
July 1910

During the next weeks Les Richman came over ever day to see Dolin, and my heart lifted when I'd hear his knock. He didn't talk much, but he was the gentlest man I ever witnessed. He would lean down to Jakie and say, "How you, Little Man?" At first Jakie would duck his head but in no time he'd warm up and tap his tin can for Les to look.

I felt at ease with Les sitting at the kitchen table while I cooked. Or he might carry a tub of wet clothes to the line and watch me pin them up. It was so hot, I even pushed the sleeves of my dress up to my elbows in front of him.

"How's Dolin?" he asked one day like always.

"He's asleep. Dr. Beale just left."

Les followed me to my room where Dolin slept. He held his hat in both hands with his eyes on Dolin, who breathed through his mouth. The skin on the left side of his face was still red. He wasn't what you call talking, just mumbling "thank ye" ever once in a while. Dr. Beale had found a break in Dolin's leg and set it, but still didn't know why the man didn't wake up enough to do more than swallow.

Les watched me give Dolin water, and then he followed me into the kitchen, where we did most of our talking. I was surprised when he said he was not a Catholic, as he was Annie's stepson.

He said, "Maw Richman's real good about not harping on me or Papa to convert—much as she wants it."

It was odd that the Richmans, nor nobody else I knew of, said anything about Les coming over, while Bertie didn't like leaving her son with me. I was still a married woman, even if Mr. Hershall and me weren't laying down like man and wife.

It relieved me to tell Les, "Mr. Hershall has kept his word these past five months. He promised that he only wanted me to take care of Jakie and his house and that's all the marriage is."

I couldn't be sure, because Les has a way of rubbing the side of his nose, but maybe I saw him smile.

Ever day around five o'clock I looked out the back window to see if Les was riding his horse up from the woods. I could usually tempt him into staying for supper and get him to talking. I was curious about his Richman family.

"My own Maw died when I was three," he said. "I don't remember her, but Maw Richman keeps her picture hanging on the wall so I can honor her memory."

He told me the names of his sisters, starting with Christina and ending with Lulie. And in between was six more kids—one a brother named Foster and one a baby boy that died at birth. "All my life, the Richmans and the Linkahans have been the tightest friends from the oldest to the littlest."

I also longed to know about Maribelle. I had seen her at a distance but not close up—John L. Meadors' daughter was a pretty little blonde and Les was courting her, but whenever I asked Les about her, his face done went dark.

"She said her maw wants her to go to that Nazareth College clear on the other side of Bardstown. So she tells me she wants to get married and us buy a farm with some riding horses. That's a dream for a richer man than me. Now, what do you think of that?"

I thought about that a lot. If Maribelle went to college she'd get all educated and never want to settle back with her people. Maybe that's what had upset Les. Or maybe he didn't want to quit working the moonshine and start in again at the sawmill. What really bothered me was how I was feeling. I'm married and I keep looking out the window for another man.

During the weeks after I signed on to take care of Dolin, I worried if I could do all Dr. Beale said. "Give him a tablespoon of laudanum when the pain gets too bad, and change the gauze on his face. Don't wrap it up, just use a saline solution and lay it wet on his face."

He didn't have to tell me to keep ever thing clean and to boil the water I used.

"And also see if you can get him to eat a little more than chicken broth."

That meant I had to run back and forth much of the time and hold a cup to Dolin's lips.

Sometimes he thrashed around and got his sheets all sweaty, but no matter—I had my biggest tin washtub filled once a day. Dolin's brothers Cleophus and Jimmy Lee would come over ever morning and haul water from the creek, and make sure the woodbox stayed full for me to boil water.

Sometimes the tub held old bandages, scalding for me to reuse; sometimes it was bed sheets. Seemed like I was always washing or hanging something on the clothesline. Good thing the July sun was hot and dried things fast.

Dolin slept a lot, but after a few days he began to talk and we could rest easy that his mind wasn't gone. When Bertie and his brothers come to see him, she was her old hateful self, even while she sat beside Dolin's bed saying her rosary. "That laudanum is opium," she sais, looking real mean at me. "You sure he won't get hooked?"

I answered nice because I knew how much she suffered seeing her oldest son in bed sick. "Dr. Beale said his medicine has to be strong to keep down the pain."

One time Bertie stayed while I was changing Dolin's dressings. "Are you doing that right?" she said. Then she jumped up crying and ran out of the house.

Emmalene
August 1910

During the first part of August, I heard Dolin moving and I went to his bedside. His eyes were wide awake and he was sitting up on the side of the bed. The skin around his left eye had peeled off and his singed eyebrow and lashes grew in white and patchy.

"Could you eat something?"

He looked at me like he didn't know who I was. Then he whispered, "If it won't be any trouble, that would be right nice."

"Does your leg hurt?" I asked. I had cut his fingernails and scrubbed his hands because he couldn't quit scratching his face.

"It's been a lot better." His lips turned up a little. He looked around. "Is this your room?"

"Yes, and little Jakie's over there sleeping sound as a stone."

I fairly skipped out to the kitchen, glad Dolin had come out of his sleeping and could eat something besides soup and wet bread.

When Bertie came later and saw him full awake, she sat holding his hand and started in asking him questions. "Son, you're better now. Can we take you on home?"

Dr. Beale told Bertie, "Don't rush things. He still needs rest. You don't want to double back on his progress, now, do you?"

Bertie stood up to go. "I'll bring him over some ham soup tonight. I know what he likes."

When she left, Dr. Beale winked at me. "Don't mind Bertie. She's one of those mothers that won't let go."

I wondered if the Catholics taught anything about kindness. My dear mother had told me, "The most important thing in this world is to help one another get through it."

But it was me being self-righteous.

Emmalene
September 1910

It was a Saturday afternoon, the 17th day of September. I had pinned back my wet hair and had stooped to wipe up spills from the wash pan. I turned around and there was Dolin holding onto the wall and walking into the kitchen. His eyes had laugh lines that made him look like he was smiling all the time, so I didn't know. Did he see me taking a bath? No, he would have let me know he was there.

"How you feeling?" I asked. I couldn't help but think he was a whole lot improved.

"I'm still kicking, but not very high." The slight pull of his wrinkled skin under his left eye gave what could be a wink. "My leg sure does itch and sting but I ought to be glad I still got it."

He sat down in a kitchen chair. "Where's Jakie?" he asked looking around.

"This time of day he's most likely in the barn or playing with the dog. Mr. Hershall sometimes keeps him close by him, but said nothing would hurt the boy because he's not smart enough to be scared of anything."

"I don't know if that's right," Dolin said. He tilted his head and looked out the window toward the sounds of a galloping horse. His voice changed, grew tense. "There comes Boone riding like the devil. Something's up."

I whirled to the doorway and Dolin struggled from the chair and followed me outside to the back yard.

Boone was wild-eyed as he rode up to the back door. The horse stamped and blowed and swooped its head in a low arc.

Boone flung himself from the saddle and took off his hat. "Emmalene, they was talk over to the store that the sheriff was fixing to raid the Old Man. Where's Les? Do you know?"

My heart thumped and I twisted my hands. "I didn't see him yet today." My head buzzed.

Dolin stood beside me, "How near by are they?"

"The talk sounded like they's right close. If Les comes here, tell him stay hid til I get back. Somebody put the word out on him working for the old man."

Boone turned to get back on his horse.

Like a bolt of lightning on a sunny day, a blast from a shotgun came from the woods. In no more than a second, we heard another shot.

"You all get back inside!" yelled Boone, "If Les ain't here, I got to find him," and he leaped on his horse and sped away.

"Jakie! Where's Jakie!" I screamed like a madwoman.

In the chicken house I found the boy holding the white hen that had a bad leg. It couldn't run, how come Jakie, slow his own self, was able to catch it. He stroked its dusty feathers.

I carried him inside where Dolin stood, then I walked out again. "I don't know what to do," I said, twisting my head so much that my hair spilled from its combs. I shaded my eyes and looked toward the place where Les and the old man worked.

Some time later Dolin and I watched Mr. Hershall's horse and wagon coming from the woods. A tarpaulin was spread over a slender mound in the bed of the wagon. A creeping fear came on me and I couldn't help but cry out, "Les!"

A uniformed man with a bulking stomach drove the wagon toward Dolin and me.

Dolin whispered close to my ear, "That's Sheriff Winters. He's the s.o.b. they send here to break up moonshines. He's a hooligan and nothing but, and when they put a badge on him, he struts like he's the Mayor of Bardstown."

I couldn't breathe. I stared at a younger man sitting beside the tarp in the bed of the wagon. Strange how my mind went to wandering. Like in a dream I was struck by the sight of the tops of the cedars along my garden fence, strung with garlands of orange horns on a trumpet vine. Dry thistle bushes held a smattering of purple blooms among brown stalks and wisps of white, blow-away seeds.

The young deputy's face warned me of what I dreaded to hear.

Sheriff Winters started talking before he stopped the wagon. "He shot first, Ma'am. You can ask all's was there and they'll tell you. He shot first."

I staggered back and Dolin grabbed my arm. I steadied myself against him to keep from falling, not thinking he might not be able to hold me up.

"What? Who?" My dry mouth wouldn't say more. Blood pounded

in my ears.

"He's dead, Ma'am. He shot first when we got there. Wasn't no call to do that!"

"What happened?" asked Dolin. He held my trembling arm.

The younger man, just a half-grown boy answered, "It's the old man."

Winters broke in, "I had my weapon drawed, but I wasn't aiming to shoot nobody. It was him that fired first and that can be proved over to the courthouse!"

I looked at the canvas-covered form in the back of the wagon. Nestled at each side were kegs and boxes of filled bottles of whiskey. From the woods came sounds of other lawmen breaking up the still, chopping holes in the copper pots, dismantling the coiled tubing, emptying the cooking mash into the stream.

When the men drove away, I turned to Dolin and looked into his troubled face. "He said they're taking Mr. Hershall's body to the coroner. That would be Dr. Beale, right?"

Dolin nodded.

"They asked me if I wanted to see his body, and I said no. Do you think that was wrong of me?"

"No, Emmalene. No."

"They claimed it was self-defense. They took all the whiskey that was made and dumped out the rest."

Dolin patted my arm.

"They said they took the whiskey as evidence. Carried it away right alongside his body."

"Emmalene, I've gotta help Les," Dolin said. "I've got to go find him."

I know Dolin left on foot, but I don't remember saying goodbye. I stared out the window not seeing. The hot still air carried the droning sound of crickets, and from the mantel in my front room, I heard the clock striking. I sat there with Jakie, barely able to get him some cornbread and milk.

I recalled Dr. Beale's words the night before. "Emmalene, I heard talk in Bardstown about the law clamping down on moonshining in these parts. Make an example out of somebody. Maybe you could carry the word to your husband to watch his stuff and look out who he fools with."

But I never got to warn Mr. Hershall. I had waited til way after supper because Les and I had sat at the table talking.

Late in the night, way after Les had gone, I remembered what Dr. Beale said. I left Dolin and Jakie asleep and carried a lantern back to the woods to give the message to Mr. Hershall.

All the sudden my old husband stood in front of me holding his shotgun like he might shoot me. Before I could explain what Dr. Beale had said, the old man yelled, "Put out that light and go on back to the house and stay there!"

I should have made him listen, but I didn't. I only turned the wick all the way down on the lantern and hurried back along the trail through the woods just like I came.

Numbness wore off a little at a time, but it wasn't until I sat alone with Jakie, grieving about where Les was, and afraid about Dolin setting out on foot and not yet healed, that shame finally came over me. I had not been worried for my husband—I had been thinking only of Les. I knew then my character was sorely lacking. And I got worse. I couldn't help but feel relief when my new situation hit me. The words shocked me when I spoke them out loud, "I'm a widow."

Les
September 1910

When I left the shine, I'd already put in a good day's work for the old man—cutting firewood, washing vats and getting lumps out of the barrel of scalded mash by pushing them through a metal sieve.

Mr. Hershall had said, "Go on home, Les. That branch water ain't flowing too pert, anyway. Just about petered out. Come late fall, it'll run steady enough." He smiled. "I'm just now storing this week's run in that holler place you dug out. The thirty-gallon keg in front is yours, whenever you get ready to take it."

"Much obliged," I said, leading my horse away. I already had another keg earned and sitting in Maw's front room.

Before I cleared the edge of the woods and stepped into the path at the edge of Emmalene's garden, I squinted my eyes toward the farmhouse kitchen. Emmalene stood at the back door with a white wrapping piled around her head. She threw a wash pan of water into a clump of goldenrod that grew beside the door.

She's busy—I won't stop by this evening.

I remembered the night before when she said she'd bake me a apple pie, but I had a feeling that a sweet, spicy pie was not what I was wanting. It was seeing her hands working and how she took care of Jakie and Dolin, how she listened to me and trusted me. I talked more with her than any other human, which would put me to shame in front of Maribelle.

They say a patient falls in love with his nurse and I worried if Dolin was plumb taken like I was.

She's married and both Dolin and me ought to put her out of mind, if not for our own sake, then for hers.

And besides, I couldn't betray the old man.

When I crossed the creek the evening sun made shiny tips on the water. How can anything look so pretty when I feel so miserable?

I had studied hard over the fix I was in, and made up my mind to talk sense to Maribelle. If she was going to college we had ought to call it quits. Besides, she knew and I knew I could not keep her in clothes and riding horses like she was used to. John L. and Retta only had the one kid and it was natural they spoil her, but that was a rich man's job and I wasn't one.

By the time I got to the Meadors' house I knew I had to tell Maribelle something, but not the truth. The truth was I loved Emmalene Hershall.

I hadn't yet dismounted, when I saw Boone galloping his horse into the Meadors' driveway. He reined in close. I didn't know what to think at his face being so pinched.

"Les, my God, ain't you heard what happened? You got to get out of here!" He breathed hard. "They's revenuers come to raid the still back yonder." He jerked his head toward the moonshine. "I was at Emmalene's back door and I heard the shots myself. And, Les, somebody told them you was working for the old man. That's why I come to carry the word."

"Is Emmalene okay?" My heart raced thinking maybe she was hurt. And then I feared what happened to the old man.

"Yeah, she's all right, but you got to catch that evening train!" Boone's eyes flared. "No telling where the sheriff's headed at right now."

Boone's horse stood stamping its feet, blowing slobber and snorting.

John L. had come out of his house and he put a hand on my shoulder. "You better go, Son. They mean to catch them somebody." He turned to Boone. "If it was me, I wouldn't go out the road—I'd get to Bardstown through the woods. It'll take twice as long, but it'll be more safe."

I closed my eyes. "I gotta go tell Maw I'm leaving."

"Too risky," said Boone. "We'll take the back trails from here, even mash down a couple of fences if we have to."

I crushed out my cigarette on a patch of bare ground. I had on work clothes with just my tobacco sack and change in my pockets.

Boone looked at me sharp. "That Sheriff Winters might look lazy, but he's getting paid plenty to catch anybody he can. He'll be searching all around here til at least dark."

Walking away from travelers near the creek, Boone and me sometimes rode, sometimes walked our horses over cow trails up and down the knobs, heading to town. The trees around us grew tall and straight up, too crowded to lean. Tiny slate rocks and twigs rolled under the horses' hooves.

Sometimes we lost the path and hiked downhill through the grass avoiding sinkholes and outcrops of rocks. We didn't talk, so the squirrels and the birds sounded louder. A buzzard floated in the sky and the treetops glowed like a painting in the sunset.

It was near dark when we got to the train depot at the far edge of Bardstown. We waited in a clump of trees in sight of the station until the northbound train pulled in.

Boone asked me to hold his horse while he walked to the office and bought me a ticket. When he got back, he said, "The news is already out. I overheerd two men come in saying Old Man Hershall was killed. You know how bad this will stir things up. They'll be making a big case out of the raid to cover their behinds about the killing."

I never seen Boone's face so troubled. He offered to trade hats. "Here. Pull this down over your eyes, and keep your head down. Just in case."

I hated hearing the old man was dead, but was overtook with my own safety. "Do you think Winters will have somebody hiding out on the train looking for me?"

"What I know of that black'ard sheriff, he won't think quick enough to do that, but no need to take a chance while you can yet be seen here in town."

"What time is it?"

"About time you was boarding. After the train pulls out of here, you can rest easy."

"I'm obliged to you."

"Don't mention it. If you want to write to your Maw or anybody, just send it to RFD #2, care of Donatus Boone. I'll open it and carry any inside letter to whoever."

"Donatus? Your name is Donatus?"

"Yeah, that's it."

"I never heard it said before."

"Well, it ain't no saint's name, but then I'm no saint neither."

"Donatus, huh?"

"Yeah. I'll tell Annie to send her mail to my Uncle Joe Elliott up in Farmington, Illinois. You tell him I sent you to work for him."

I handed my horse's reins to Boone. "I ask a favor of you. Would you dig up my 30-gallon keg of whiskey if it's still hid?" I told him exactly where I had dug out a holler behind a twin trunk maple close to the old man's still. "And tell Maw I wanted to see her bad before I left."

"I'll sure do it, and I'll smooth it over with her. Now go and get on that train. You've got a long trip."

I reached out and gave Boone a handshake and felt a wad of bills closed into my fist.

"For the whiskey," Boone said, his eyes shiny.

I nodded, stretched the hat down tighter and walked toward the train platform. The conductor shouted, "All aboard!" The whistle shrieked. I felt my heart twist as I thought about the old man laying dead, and me leaving Emmalene and Landing Run. I worried about what Maw would think the next afternoon, and the next, and every time hereafter when she heard the lonesome high-pitched cry of the train.

Emmalene
September 1910

The morning after Mr. Hershall was killed, I walked around the house not seeing or hearing. Dr. Beale came by to fill out the coroner's report.

"Do you want me to have Mr. Hershall's body brought back here for the showing?"

I pondered his meaning.

"The mortician in Bardstown can be here early tomorrow morning, if you want to hold a wake here in your house."

I nodded slow. "Yes," I said, at last. "It's fitting he be laid in the family plot where his pa and ma are." Then I remembered more graves were there. "And his first wife and those little babies they lost."

As Dr. Beale stood up to leave, I had a worry. "I don't know where Mr. Hershall kept his money…"

"Don't you fret, Emmalene. Details can be worked out when you've got your wits straightened out."

My life was different and gonna get more different. I'd have to find out what all money was in the bank, or if it was hid, to pay out for the funeral and everything else from now on.

Dr. Beale told me that Dolin was home, not getting much rest, but home. So I was surprised to see Bertie right in there with Miz Annie and the other women when they come over to clean house.

Miz Annie said, "Now, Emmalene, the Women's Sodality from over to church always scrubs the house of the dead so you can have a peaceful burial. All you have to do is show us where your mop and cleaning rags are."

It seemed funny to me that the sickbed they were scouring was not from the man who died, but from Dolin who had slept there for a good two months.

Those women looked around everywhere and I couldn't blame them. The Hershalls had never let any Catholics enter the farmhouse, so it was the first time in at least eighty-four years that any in Landing Run knew what was inside.

At least the Sodality could see my rooms was already scrubbed. The biggest thing in my kitchen was the black stove with four curved iron legs. So big and tall it took up the whole wall between two windows. I had blackened it the first week I moved here. When I cooked I had hot water in a side reservoir and a warming oven over top.

Dishes was few. I had a small set of blue enamel ware from Rice's that I kept stacked on the kitchen table, along with a couple open jars of jelly and jam.

When the old man brought me to this house I had sought out the reason for so little sign of his dead wife. Elizabeth Fielding was my step-father Everett Fielding's sister, but he had never talked much about her since she had left Clay County many years before and died in Nelson. Was it her didn't keep a good house—there being only a water bucket, a skillet, a coffee pot and some tin cups and plates? No figurines or pictures, not a set of dishes in the cupboard or a apron hanging on a hook. Nothing homey. Mr. Hershall had said his father built the house—only why wasn't much of anything left over from all those years? Or was Mr. Hershall so tore up with grief that he threw out reminders of her?

Then too, maybe the old man sold the stuff. I wouldn't put it past him, close as he was to his money.

Three of the women pulled the feather tick off my bed, and threw it across the clothesline for a good beating and airing. Some of them set in to scrubbing and whitening the walls with a limestone wash while some cooked, bringing food from their homes. They didn't let me work as to getting anything ready for the next day's wake and funeral the day after.

Miz Annie stayed right close and I had the feeling she was protecting me. As a Greenhaven that married a Richman, she was part of two of the oldest families that had settled Landing Run, and that gave her top standing with the women in my house.

"Garr's people helped build one of the first forts against the Indians in Bardstown, and my family was part of the Catholics that came from St. Mary's County in Maryland," said Miz Annie. "We had this land here all this time, so you know it hurt when…"

She stopped talking and I knew it was about the cornfield. Before I could give my regrets over Mr. Hershall buying it, I remembered, "Now, I own it."

Miz Annie went right in to telling me something personal. "You know, my sister Retta did wrong by me. She could of easy lent us the money to pay up the lien against our house so we wouldn't needed to sell the land in the bottoms!"

I kept my head down while we changed pillowcases and smoothed the fresh sheets. I had not slept in the bed since Dolin left; instead, I kept to the pallet outside the room. Something about running my hands over the goose-feathered mattress, made me think of Les. It wasn't right. I was not mourning my husband; I was aching for the loss of another man, Miz Annie's son.

"I know John L. would have come to our aid, but he always lets Retta boss him." Miz Annie talked on. "I know her. She probably said, 'We cannot loan out our hard-earned money to those that can't repay us, family or no!' And here we were, this close to foreclosure from the bank." Miz Annie put her thumb to the tip of her forefinger.

It was no wonder I got nervous when Retta and Maribelle Meadors stopped by. Both were dressed up like going to town, not cleaning house.

It was a Sunday and all the other women had gone home from Mass first to change into ever day clothes. I know Catholics aren't supposed to work on Sunday, but Miz Annie explained. "Sometime they's work has to be done, Sunday or no. I'm sure our dear Lord understands."

Retta wore a two-piece dark green outfit with rows of buttons down the sleeves to both wrists. She took off her brown hat and its speckled feathers waved.

When Miz Annie said she had to go home, Retta grabbed her arm. "You most certainly cannot go…I just got here!" She didn't act like anything was wrong between them.

I was took aback when I stood up close to Maribelle and saw how she was only a girl. I remembered that Les told me she was eighteen. She was dressed fine, too, in a ecru dress with lace on a high neck collar, flounced petticoats and calf street boots with tall arches.

At least Maribelle thought to pay her respects. "I'm sorry about your loss."

Then Retta popped up, "If there's anything we can do…" And her voice trailed off while she looked around my living room.

I was that proud of what I had fixed up. There wasn't much furniture and the tall ceilings made it look even more bare. But I had polished the wood floor, shined up the lamp chimney, and crocheted the edges of my white spreads. I found a little glass vase to hold flowers of their season and put it all on the walnut table. When it was moved under the window it looked right fancy in the sunlight.

On one side of the fireplace I had a rocking chair that Mr. Hershall had brought down for me from the locked room upstairs, and Jakie had his little stool.

They wasn't much I could do with Mr. Hershall's brass spittoon and his high-backed horsehair chair on the other side of the fireplace. But here again, these were changes I could make. All is mine to decide, now.

As the women were leaving for home, I overheard Maribelle. "Aunt Annie, the reason I didn't go to Nazareth yet is I haven't heard from Les. I wrote him a seven-page letter, front and back, would you mail it for me?"

Miz Annie frowned but she took the fat envelope and put it in her apron pocket.

That letter haunted me, 'specially when Miz Annie said she was spending the night. "This is a hard time for you, Emmalene. You need another woman's company."

When we sat down to talk, Miz Annie said, "Les didn't even get to tell me bye." Her broken voice told me how much she hurt to have him gone, hiding from the law.

I wanted to ask about Les, but it didn't seem right, not with my husband not yet buried and now that I was sitting so close to Maribelle's letter in Miz Annie's pocket. What does she think of Maribelle seeing Les? They're not kin because Les is Annie's stepson, but does Miz Annie see anything in such of a girl to make a good wife for him?

The next morning, the wind was easy blowing and dew shined on the grass in the rising sunlight. I found it strange to feel so happy and I thought maybe I shouldn't.

I put on my best dress. "I know it ain't black or silk but do you think it's okay?"

Miz Annie nodded big and smiled. Yet I know she can't see very good, for she held ever thing up close to her eyes when she fixed Jakie his milk and mush and dressed him in his good shirt and overalls.

When Garr came for Miz Annie to get her home for to change her dress, Jakie took off his shoes and padded to the barn lot to scrape circles in the dirt with a small hickory branch. I let him go. Lord, I'll not disturb him any more than I have to.

Before nine o'clock, I heard wheels crunching gravel in the back driveway. Behind Dr. Beale's buggy rolled the black-painted funeral wagon, its team of horses driven by the undertaker from Bardstown. He had one helper.

Dr. Beale introduced me to the two gloomy men dressed in black suits and then he pointed to a spot in front of the cold fireplace. "Is this where you'd like him laid out?"

I nodded and moved Mr. Hershall's chair out of the way.

The mortician and his worker crept around in soft shoes setting up the bier, then went to the casket wagon and brought in the flat-topped box covered with a charcoal gray cloth. As they passed through the door, I stood back and closed my eyes.

"I picked out a plain coffin," Dr. Beale said, taking off his driving gloves. "Pine box. Something I thought Mr. Hershall would approve. It's simple, got cotton padding and a black linen cloth lining."

Finally I looked at the lid, scared I would see inside the box.

"I bought him a new suit coat. Black. And a white shirt. Nothing fancy. Except the tie has little flowers down it. Cheery."

"I can't thank you enough," I said. I doubted the old man had ever before wore a suit, much less a tie. But it didn't matter. I had decided not to have a open casket, knowing Mr. Hershall wouldn't want the people he hated staring at his dead face, saying, "Don't he look natural."

"No need for thanks, Emmalene. When a doctor can't do anything more for the living, at least he should help out with the dead." Dr. Beale took off his coat. "By the way, Boone didn't want it told, but he came in and paid for everything."

"He did?" My eyes opened wide.

"Don't worry, he's got the money. You know he owns that big hog farm and, across the road, a piece of land with the empty cabin—next one over from your place. I guess he's showing appreciation for all the good whiskey he's bought from the old man over the years."

I thought I saw the doctor wink. Has he heard about me being in that cabin with Albert? I never knew when he was kidding. He took his timepiece from a vest pocket, pulled it toward his face, and then pushed it away. The loops of gold chain sparkled as they bounced across his chest. "I'd say there'll be a good wake here, today, when the neighbors pile in."

"Even though Mr. Hershall wasn't Catholic?"

I poured another cup of coffee for Doctor. He relaxed, stretched his legs under the table, his pointed-toe boots gleaming.

"I sent a telegram to what's left of the Hershall family in the mountains," he said, "but I never got a return answer."

As I stood over his right shoulder, I smelled brilliantine in his hair and noticed the bald spot at the top of his head. I looked around the kitchen for places to sit. Just the two straight chairs that him and me were using. People think Mr. Hershall is rich. Won't they be surprised to see what little furniture they is in such a big house.

I couldn't help but think how the old man would be mad as a hornet if he knew the Catholics were coming, again—even more this time.

By noon, families were filling the drive with buggies and wagonloads of kids. First thing, the boys took off their shoes, forgot their slicked down hair and clean overalls. The little girls walked careful trying not to muss their starched dresses with tied sashes.

Eliza Boone carried a plate of fried chicken in one hand and boiled ham in the other. Annie and her daughters, Christina and Nan Mary, brought in cornbread and bowls of green beans, mashed potatoes and slaw.

At the coffin, Boone and Garr took off their hats and mumbled something, then stood silent, looking at the closed top. Boone bowed his head. After a minute Boone went outside and brought in two long benches he'd borrowed from church and set them along the walls in the viewing room.

The women in Landing Run had never been so nice. I nodded at each one's consoling, while their niceness washed over me. I could tell that some of them was disappointed in not seeing the old man's face in death, but I knew I made the right decision about keeping the coffin closed.

In my kitchen, the tabletop disappeared under overlapping bowls of garden vegetables swimming in yellow butter and fatback. A young husband, in tight-fitting overalls and a vest, brought in the two cane-backed chairs from the front porch and placed a smooth plank across them to hold the pies—custard, apple and mincemeat.

"Nothing special," said Miz Annie, but I thought it a feast.

The Catholics fascinated me. They gazed at the coffin and whispered their prayers, and then made the sign of the cross, barely skimming their forehead, breastbone, and both shoulders. One old man tapped his chest three times and was done.

The Linkahans arrived, but Dolin wasn't with them. Bertie walked behind her son, Cleophus, who carried a small wooden crate covered with a tea towel. The mother of all the boys seemed to have trouble lifting her eyes to mine when I held open the kitchen door.

"My sympathy," said Bertie, in a low voice. "I've brought a jam cake."

Cleophus beamed, his smile quietly embracing me.

Bertie tipped her head to the women in the kitchen then said to me, "Dolin sends his regards. He'll come to the burying tomorrow, but I didn't want him over-tired."

Boone, his voice solemn, interrupted at the back door. "Is there a special place back yonder where you want us to dig, Emmalene?" He motioned his head toward the family graveyard in the woods beyond the farm buildings.

"If you would, just pick out a nice spot. Mr. Hershall caught me up there once and said he didn't want me traipsing around. I'm not right sure I could find the place, again."

"I got an idea about where. It won't be no trouble," said Boone. He called to the boys and they swaggered, chins in the air, as they helped Boone pull shovels, a pick ax, and trenching tools from his wagon.

Someone hung a funeral wreath on the front door, its shiny black ribbons twining around a circle of twisted grapevines. Scarlet sumac leaves was tucked between sprigs of goldenrod and purple asters.

My face grew soft with pleasure. "It's beautiful," I said.

Nan Mary Richman's voice tinkled like silver bells, "Christina and me made it!"

Christina looked to be about fifteen or sixteen. She hung her head, while a pleased smile spread across her tanned face.

The girls were Les's sisters and my heart filled at their tenderness. The whole day put me in the mind of a party, but even so, it sure was exhausting.

Miz Annie made me sit down on the front porch and gave me a glass of sweet tea and a thick sandwich. "At least eat some of Eliza's ham!"

"People at the store used to say Mr. Hershall was quare-turned. He didn't want anybody here, so why you suppose they all come in now that he's dead?"

"The old man didn't have much to do with anybody except to sell his likker. But, Emmalene, it don't matter if he was a standoffish mountaineer and a non-Catholic to boot. Nobody'll soon forget the kindness you showed when you took care of Dolin."

"I just did what any of you all would."

"Don't you see? Folks are paying you their respects. They've come to let you know how they feel, without saying."

I smiled and blinked several times. I hoped that if Mr. Hershall looked at us from a world beyond, he would be more understanding of the neighborhood, wouldn't be mad that I had let them in. He once told me that his paw and mama, his first wife Elizabeth Fielding and three of their still-born babies were buried in the family graveyard. Maybe he would be at ease when we put him to rest beside those who truly loved him.

"I reckon it's a good-sized funeral," said Miz Annie. "Garr counted about three dozen come." She and husband Garr and Boone and Eliza had sat up all night with Mr. Hershall's corpse while I slept. My bed smelled like sunshine and lavender and I was out for eight hours. It had been a long time since I could sleep straight through without checking on Dolin needing something, or because of recounting my troubles.

The little Hershall graveyard plot was filled with people. The women wore either black or gray dresses and the young'uns had on their best. The girls had pinned black bows onto their bodices and braided black ribbons into their hair. Some of them had small bunches of flowers. I looked down at the black dress Miz Rice brought over for me to wear. I had tied a wide black sash around the middle to make it fit better, and I stitched a thin piece of black gauze on the brim of my hat to cover my face.

White paling fenced in the small graveyard where we stood and grass grew over sunken shapes, small ones for Mr. Hershall's first three little babies that all died before Jakie's papa Big Jake was born. A tombstone within a few feet of the open grave read, "ELIZABETH FIELDING HERSHALL, Wife and Mother, 1835—1898."

Annie stood next to me, where somebody already put up a smooth rock, carved "Notice Hershall Jr. Born Sept. 25, 1825. Just recent, somebody had added, "Died September 17, 1910." I figured Mr. Hershall had carved the stones hisself, and I puzzled over who carved the death date.

Retta and Maribelle were behind us with Retta moving her rosary beads through her fingers, her lips mouthing the words, her head turning from side to side. I heard Retta whisper, "Old Man Hershall likened eight days of being eighty-five year old."

When everybody was gathered round, our shoes crunching the dead leaves and acorns, Boone got the young pallbearers to carry the coffin from the funeral wagon.

Boone said, "Set it down easy, boys."

Of course, the priest from Our Lady of Hope wasn't there, and everybody stood silent for a while.

I was glad when Dr. Beale spoke. "Notice Hershall wasn't a Catholic and he had some hard ways. He was a loner and an outsider, but he minded his own business, never cheated anybody, and he never wasted nature."

If truth be told, the men standing there in white shirts, some in suit coats, some in clean overalls, were probably saying, "And he made some darn good whiskey." I turned my gaze to Boone, Garr, John L. and Dr. Beale, all with heads down, holding their hats. I bet they would praise the old man's memory as time went by.

Dr. Beale wound up his remarks. "He left a wife and a grandson, and we join together to say the prayer common to all of us. 'Our Father, who art in Heaven, hallowed be Thy name...'"

A breeze stirred giving that first true feel of autumn. Treetops swayed gentle-like, leaves curled up at the edges and thunder rumbled way off. I felt real peaceful listening to voices lifting for my old dead husband. I stood there quiet, holding Jakie's hand, trying to keep him from swinging our arms back and forth.

Behind me I heard Eliza Boone say to Bertie, "Oh, how will she take care of that little boy?"

I worried if others, too, thought I could not do for him or manage the farm.

After the coffin was let down, Miz Annie walked me outside the paling fence. She stayed while the other women walked past me, each one saying something. I heard some woman in the back whisper loud, "She don't look like she's taking it too hard." At first I suspicioned I didn't hear right, but I couldn't ask Annie who had already bid me goodbye.

Was it Bertie said that? Would she slight me right as I buried my husband's corpse? I made myself a promise that if I ever got the chance, I was going to tell her I did not do anything wrong with Albert. Would that help her opinion of me?

It was then I saw Dolin. He walked with a cane and limped over to speak to me. He stood close enough I could see his burned left eyebrow was growing back in white, not red. The skin around his eye pulled somewhat like he was all time winking. It wasn't awful, and not so strange since he already had laugh wrinkles.

"Emmalene, I'll walk you and Jakie back to your house."

I looked, but Bertie had gone.

"It's right nice of you to show your sympathies, but are you sure you ought to be outdoors so long?"

Dolin took my arm and I matched my steps to his. I could hear back at the grave, the shovels of dirt thrown in. I turned around and the last of the mourners was leaving. One young woman stood still, staring at Dolin and me. It was Christina Richman.

I hadn't gone nowhere outside the farm since July 18 when the sawmill blew and Dolin came to stay. Not even to Rice's Store to return the mourning clothes Miz Rice lent me. Maybe I ought to keep the black dress and wear it a few months and pay it off in egg money.

I thought sooner or later I would feel like a sad widow, but I didn't. In fact I felt free, like a heavy hand had quit pushing me down. I didn't want a black dress to remind me how things was before.

"Come on inside, Jakie," I said, calling the boy to eat his supper. That's when Boone come riding up.

He got off his horse and dug into his saddlebag. His voice was low. "Me and the boys bought up the whiskey Les buried for the old man. It was quite a lot and the law never found it because Les hid it good under where them twin oaks grow."

I was surprised by the brownish envelope and felt my shoulders sag. I had not known the weight I carried over having no money.

"Would you care for some beans and cornbread? Jakie's fixing to eat," I said.

"Thankee, no, but here's something else. "I just come from the mail boxes at the store."

Boone held out a small white envelope with just the word "Emmalene" written on the front.

"It's from Les?" I asked, knowing that it had come in an outside envelope addressed to Boone.

Boone nodded, tipped his hat and got back on his horse.

"I can't advise sending a answer back, Emmalene. I've seen government men snooping around the store, writing things down. But I'll let you know when all's clear," he said, and rode away.

My heart beat with excitement as I put off opening the triple folded paper. As long as I hadn't read it yet, I could dream about what it said.

I took my time getting Jakie to the table. "Come on now. Let's wash your little face and hands."

I put some warm bean soup in a bowl and crumbled cornbread on top. I dipped cold milk from a stone crock that I'd brought from the springhouse and poured a glass for Jakie.

By that time I was wild to read the letter.

>Sep 21 1910
>Dear Emmalene,
>   I take pen in hand to say this finds me safe and well.
>   I got working right away on the farm with Boone's uncle and he's a square dealer. It don't pay so good but I live cheap so I can send postal orders home to Maw. That suits for now.
>   Emmalene I am heartsick over your hard luck. Mr. Hershall sure was fair with me and I got to know him pretty good. I am sorry I could not give you my sympathy before I had to leave. How does little Jakie take it? What do you hear from Dolin? I reckon he has gone back home.
>   Well I have a million questions about the old home place but guess I better stop this scribbling and close my eyes. Farmers gets up awful early.

I would treasure to get a letter back from you—to hear your side and ever thing.
    Your friend,
    Les Richman

I read the letter twice and then folded it into my apron pocket among my clothes pins. I leaned my head over and pressed my fingers against my eyes. I feared letting my feelings completely out, for sobs that great would scare Jakie.

What's the matter with me? Did I miss something in the letter? I read it again, turning each page over and over. As nice as the words read, something was missing. I wished for more but what?

Jakie was happy with his food and I ran to the barn, and let myself fall into a pile of hay. A disturbed chicken squawked, ruffled its feathers and hurried outside. I felt the prickle of the hay, and its dry-weed smell filled my nose. When I pulled my apron over my face, the wooden clothespins spilled out of the pockets making hollow sounds as they bounced against each other. I held onto the letter and cried until my stomach ached and my eyes burned. I couldn't come up with any answer for what had caused me to let go.

Les
September 1910

It's a good thing I farmed all the daylight hours, for at night I sat in the bunkhouse smoking and staring out the window at the dark. I had got one short letter from Boone telling me Old Man Hershall was buried and there was a investigation going on about who worked with him. And I must stay here for the time being. It's hard work gathering in crops for Boone's Uncle Joe, and he feeds us good, but it ain't home and I worried too much about what was going on in Landing Run. I feared I'd never hear from any of the rest of them. And all at once I got three letters in one envelope. And it was a fat envelope come in Boone's handwriting.

I saw right off that Maw's letter and mine had crossed in the mail and there weren't none from Emmalene. And God have mercy on me, I read Maw's letter first hoping she would mention her.

> September 21 1910 – Wed morn
> Dear Son,
>   Hope this letter finds you well as can be expected when so far yonder from home. We are fine. You know your papa has the rheumatism so bad he has to get out of the wagon when the road jounces him too much.
>   Well Christina just turned sixteen and a young woman. All us misses their son and big brother. That Sheriff Winters sent two men around here this morning asking questions. You will laugh. The little kids was outside playing Moonshine, and the two revenuers rode up to the door where I was churning butter on the porch.

I got inside and set on that keg you left here a month ago for your first pay from Old Man Hershall. Grandmaw answered the door. Bless her heart, she said she wasn't scared. I just sat there with my skirts and apron covering that keg while they searched the house. They was polite, scraping boots on doormat and looking like they rather be someplace else. They even looked in the attic. Pulled the rope down and climbed up. For the first time I was glad you was gone.

Well Christina is fixing dinner and you know she wants me to bake the biscuit. I guess you know we buried Old Man Hershall. It was yesterday morning. Emmalene is fine. She is a mighty sweet girl. Dolin is better and better. Christina saw him walking Emmalene and little Jakie home after the burying.

You take care of yourself and hope you can come back home soon. Well I have to get this carried out to Boone to take out and mail at Rice's.

From the one who loves you best,
Mother

All I could do was picture Dolin walking Emmalene home. She is a widow now and nothing to stop her and Dolin from courting. Not even Bertie.

There was many more pages I could see was from Maribelle.

Dear Les,

Hope this letter finds you in good health and good spirit. I miss you every day even if we wasn't getting along so good when you left. Papa said he is talking to the big shots at Bardstown to see what is what.

Mama and me went to every store they had over to Bardstown on Saturday and you should see what all she bought me. First a light brown winter coat with full shoulder sleeves and a dark brown band just below the elbow and long buttoned gloves to completely cover my hands and arms. And a dark purple hat with a big wide brim, piped with velvet braid and crimpled netting and some red and blue bird feather plumes and dress boots with high heels. And two dresses, one a blue suit with a silk brocade collar on the jacket

I figured back. Saturday she was out buying clothes when the old man was killed and I had to sneak out of town, for God knows how long. I skimmed through the other pages and found a one-page note from Boone.

>Sept 22
>Dear Les,
>   Am writing to say howdy but don't answer back. Agents has been snooping around here asking questions about you to the Rices and who all gets mail at the boxes out front. I reckon they mean to jail them somebody to throw off the old man being killed. I will tell your maw and them not to write you til all is safe and I won't either.
>   Your friend,
>   Boone

Well, I had already wrote to Maw and Emmalene. And now I would not get a answer.

I pondered what I should've said to Emmalene. I should have told her how I loved it when she opened her door and smiled big up at me, and how she'd pour my coffee and grin when I'd say, "Whoa." I liked it when she looked all serious-like studying how to sling the blanket up over her horse, and how her face got pink when she pounded the butter dash in a hurry for it to come butter, how she tousled Jakie's hair when she passed by his chair. I wanted to say how I wished she was my wife and I'd be proud to ride up anybody's driveway with her sitting in the buggy beside me and walk in any store in any town with her on my arm. And if I could just lay eyes on her last thing at night and first thing come morning, I'd give all I own or hope to own.

I felt like a wagon was sitting on my chest and I hung my head. They say it hurts more when a man can't cry and I reckon as how they's right.

The day after I got to Fulton County, Illinois, and Boone's Uncle Joe's farm, I went in to gathering hay with the crew. I was hitching up a mule to the wagon when Amos Young, one of the old boys said to me, "That mule's face and your'n got a lot in common."

The rest of the men stood there kind of sniggering and looking to see how I'd take it. I said back real quick, "Maybe so, but that mule's behind would make you a Sunday face."

They fell into laughing and slapping each other and me on the back. I guess they learned not to mess with a good ol' Kentucky boy.

I liked the smell of the alfalfa hay already cut and laying spread out in the field drying in the sun. Some of the men gathered and stacked it and some hay was packed into bales to haul to the barn. When Uncle Joe saw that I was strong for my size, wiry and able to handle fifty- and sixty-pound bales, he had me lifting them up into the loft for feeding his stock during the winter.

I liked working hard, sweating and grunting to keep my mind off things at home, for the sting was already on me and I was bound to make the best of the situation and get it over with.

Maw Richman's letter had said Dolin walked Emmalene home from the graveyard. I pictured him all doe-eyed sitting at her table where I used to, talking and grinning at her. I couldn't hold it against him 'cause I'd be doing more than that if only I could. I hated how the Old Man had been shot and killed, but I couldn't hide the truth from myself. It pleased me to think that now she was a widow and free to court and marry.

I groaned out loud when I thought about her being with Dolin. He had always favored her looks even before he met her down at the creek. He told me how he heard her screaming Jakie's name when the little feller got hung on a branch and threatened to fall in the water. He said, "I helped her up from where she sank onto the ground, and I could feel her skin through her dress, soft and sweet."

I couldn't stand him telling me again about how pleasing she was. Dolin is a easy-going man and it wasn't hard to switch off to ask how he liked his Uncle James in Owensboro come to court his maw.

But I didn't expect what he told me.

"It was one day in March, not long after Little Wyman was born," he said, his face losing the smile he wore all time. "Maw was in the yard visiting with Miz Retta who was out for a buggy ride."

The look on Dolin's face made me stand still and listen.

"I found a open letter on the kitchen table and looked at it. Maw was writing to Uncle James."

I had a mind to stop Dolin from telling me ever what it was, but I saw he needed to say it.

"He always was sending us big boxes by train at Christmas, filled with apples and nuts and new shoes and toys for all us. He felt sorry, us not having much of anything and him with a good business operation and no kids himself on account of Aunt Mary's poor health."

Then Dolin told me what his mother was writing in the letter.

"She called him, 'Dearest One' and thanked him for the money he sent when the baby was born. Then she told him she hoped Mary's death last year and Papa's dying after that wasn't God's judgment on them. She said exactly, '...for what we done so long ago.'"

I shook my head, not knowing what to say.

It was curious—Dolin didn't look sad. I guess he had got over the shock. I studied the woods behind him, waiting for him to go on.

"That's not all, Les, for Maw also wrote that all her boys thinks a lot of him, especially me and she's glad, since I am his son, not Wyman's."

I studied for a minute. "You didn't know any of this?"

"Papa always teased that I looked more like Uncle James than him, but I didn't know the truth of the matter and I don't think Papa did neither. It appears like Uncle James already knew some time ago."

Getting in the hay gave me plenty of time to think about Dolin and how his mother might be marrying his real father, but ever thing just led back to me grieving over Emmalene and home.

It was late September and I looked out over the flat stubble fields of dried weeds. I couldn't help but think about Landing Run with its rocky hillsides filled with bright colored trees and smelling like dried sage and hickory nuts. I could hear the creek water, spilling over rocks and twigs and rushing—where to, it didn't know.

Emmalene
September 1910

About a week after the funeral, I gathered up Mr. Hershall's overalls and bedclothes that I'd washed so I could store them away clean in a box. I scrubbed his spittoon and moved all including his hat and pipe into his room under the stairs.

Out the front window I could see the maples and sweet gums just flaming red, and the beeches was yellow. Usually something bright in nature will uplift me, but I felt aimless and empty. I talked to Jakie, my riding horse, the dog that stayed around the barn, the cow and my chickens, but nobody answered back. At times Jakie had a question on his baby face and I had a thought he missed his grandpaw.

I wasn't yearning for Mr. Hershall; I wished for some of the company I'd got used to whiles I was taking care of Dolin and during the funeral and all. The days had gone dull again. Is this how it'll be from now on?

Late in the afternoon, I was downright glad to look out and see Dr. Beale come driving his buggy around to the back. Ever body seemed to want to come in by the kitchen door.

"The mortician said this was in Mr. Hershall's pockets," and Doctor handed me a bulky envelope.

He declined my offer of coffee. "I have to be going. Got some patients to check on before dark."

I fished in the envelope and found a bandanna, a jackknife and a pocket watch, but best of all I found Mr. Hershall's ring of keys! Now, I could look in ever corner of the locked room upstairs.

The room wasn't jam-packed, yet full enough with the first Mrs. Hershall's stuff. In one corner was a four-foot long captain's trunk with leather straps, brass hinges and the whole thing was studded with rivet heads. A bed, clothes press, and baby cradle was stacked against the same side of the room. Inside the drawers of a dresser was some vases and a set of white dishes trimmed in a green vine, all wrapped in dresser scarves, aprons and tea towels. Maybe Mr. Hershall had hid his wife's things not wanting any other woman to use them.

Covered in burley sacks and standing in a corner was family portraits, but I couldn't make out who they were. Scattered about on the other side of the room was a spinning wheel, a quilting frame, and boxes of canning jars. There was another smaller hump-backed wooden trunk that I opened, but it was so dusty I brought it downstairs to clean off before I looked through it.

It was clothes that smelled old and some of the material tore apart when I picked it up. I found a hat wrapped in moldy tissue paper, but after I brushed the maroon brim real good, it looked passable.

In the bottom of the trunk I found a old yellow envelope. There was a name on it written all fancy and back-slanted in brownish ink: "Mrs. Joseph Cutler, Fairfield Kentucky."

At the top of the first sheet was written "September 1." I studied back to the funeral when I saw Mr. Hershall's Ma and Papa's tombstones, his mother being Patience Cutler Hershall born 1808, died Sept. 25, 1825. I was holding a letter written by my old husband's mother, just weeks before she died. I felt I was going into a different world when I began to read.

> Dearest Mama,
> I take pen in hand to write you a few lines today in hopes we can be reunited. I know you were crying when Papa grabbed your arm and made you get in the buggy that day when I visited church to see you. He was so angry, he pretended I wasn't there and is keeping to his threat, "If a daughter of mine marries a non-Catholic, then she will not be spoken of again by this family!" I can see him now and I cry every time I remember, for my heart is broken.
> But I feel like I am married just the same as you and Papa are married and even if Notey is a non-Catholic we might have married in the church instead of by a Justice of the Peace if Papa had not turned him away from our house. I met Notey (his full name is Notice Hershall and he is from eastern Kentucky) as he was trimming the grounds at St. Michael's Church when I was visiting Miranda. And I fell in love with him and

invited him myself to our Harvest Day dinner at home. But Papa shamed him when he turned him away, and Notey is proud like Papa and will never forget.

I am so miserable, Mama. I don't know if Miranda or her mother told you, but I am going to have a child pretty soon and I wish I could have the solace of my dear Mother here with me. For I have not been doing very well.

Notey had built a one-room cabin for us to live in Landing Run, a few miles south of Bardstown, after we married on Christmas Day. He found out how to build this house by copying from the prettiest and biggest he ever saw. Then he talked to a man who knows how to carpenter, and the rest he just figures as he goes along. We only have two rooms to live in yet. At first, all we owned was piled up in the kitchen. But after he built a real bed for us and a cradle for the baby, he had to finish another room to put them in. When he is not hoeing the corn or digging up rocks or tending the horse and cow, he is finishing our house. It sets in a grove of trees where it cuts off a lot of the wind and rain. I would be so happy, Mama, except for losing my dear parents and little brother.

Mrs. Brent, a midwife from further down in Landing Run, visited me today. She is nice, and said she will help me when my time comes. She says my morning sickness has lasted too long but she is giving me a medicine that she boils up from leaves, bark and roots she gathers in the woods. She said I am gaining all my weight in baby and losing my own body weight and I must eat more. I do try, but food gags me.

Another family is building a place in Landing Run, although we can't see each other's houses, all living among the trees on flat-topped little hills. Even if we were the type to visit our neighbors, I do not feel well enough to walk over to meet them. Notice is so stubborn, he feels like the whole neighborhood looks down on him, them all being Catholic and him not. They all seem to be kin to each other too, and that leaves us out again.

Mama, I am sick a big part of every day. I told Mrs. Brent to make sure that if it's a boy to name it Notice Hershall, Jr., and if it's a girl, to name it after you. I told her the baby must be baptized in secret because Notey would never agree to it if he knew. She must do this for me. I made her promise.

Please come to see me. God knows that Notice and I are right to be together and I am still your only daughter,
With more love than tongue can tell,
Patience.

My eyes were stinging by the time I got to the end. If Mrs. Brent kept her promise to Patience, then my old husband, Notice Hershall, Jr., was a baptized Catholic. Did he even know it? Also, my heart filled for the woman about my own age, knowing I had something in common with her. She was shut off because her husband wasn't a Catholic and I was shut off because I weren't. It doesn't seem right when all the young mother had done was to love somebody.

Emmalene
October 1910

October frost had come in and nipped the maple trees bright red. I stood at the henhouse door scattering ground corn to my flock and thinking about the folks in the mountains. They'd soon be hitching up horses and mules to the wagon and gathering up their hillside corn. Mr. Hershall had a field planted in corn and maybe I could get Dolin's brothers to bring it in.

My garden had pretty much gone to ruin after I quit tending it, but I had the pantry floor covered with white potatoes and sweet potatoes to dry. I had braided the tops of my onions together and hung them from the rafters in my kitchen. I still had squash to gather and turnips and cabbage to dig separate holes for, put them in, cover with straw, then dirt. I'd have them to eat on all winter.

Way down the lane, somewhat hid by wild wheat growing along the road, I saw a rider coming at an easy canter. I didn't know who the man was, but he sure rode proud, sitting tall in his saddle. The nearer he got, the fancier his clothes looked. He had on a blue pinstriped suit and I could see a starched white collar high around his neck.

He called out when his prancing horse got closer, "Mrs. Hershall?"

He knew my name!

"I'm Emmalene Hershall."

He brought his horse to a standstill, and swirled off his black derby hat. In the sun it showed a silk band.

"Winston Judd McPherson, from Judd, Smith, and McPherson."

I wiped a sleeve across my forehead, embarrassed about my dirty apron and work shoes up side his tailoring. I flushed when he looked at my upraised arm, bare to the elbow.

"I've come as a representative of our firm," he said, stepping from the saddle, "to read you some of the pertinent sections of your late husband's will."

"You a lawyer?" I asked, my mind spinning for the trouble lawyers usually brings, yet, I couldn't help admiring him from his shiny-buttoned shoes to his thick waves of brown hair parted down the middle. As he stepped closer I got a whiff of his talc mixed so sweet with the smell of falling leaves and nuts from the trees around us.

"Excuse my looks," I said. "I didn't know you were coming."

"Don't mind that," he said. He smiled and kept looking from my face to my bare arm.

"Come on inside," I said, stepping to the back door. I turned and watched him tie his horse's reins to the garden post. He stood for a minute looking at the dark purple berries on the pokeweed bushes growing ten-feet high, while I gaped at his trouser legs tapered down to narrow bottoms and his golden wedding ring twinkling in the sun.

I decided the man was a dandy. I was filled with wonder not only at the way he dressed, but also by the outline of his strong jaw and chin. He twitched his full lips up and down and I eased somewhat when I saw his curly-ended mustache hairs was tickling his nose.

What in the world is he doing here? I walked into the kitchen while he held the door for me. I could feel his eyes scanning me up and down.

Jakie sat behind the cooking stove, dipping a shoestring in and out a empty glass jar. He didn't even look up.

"This must be young Jake, Mr. Hershall's grandson?"

I nodded and before I could offer to take my visitor into the front room, he plopped down in a kitchen chair and dropped his cowhide satchel on the table.

"Would you like some coffee?" I asked.

I saw him gazing at a jug of buttermilk cooling in a bucket of water in the sink.

"Could I get you a glassful?" I offered.

He said yes, and I felt him watching me reach into the cupboard. "Does your wife ever churn butter?" I asked.

What a foolish question, I thought when he shook his head and chuckled. A lawyer's wife, a woman surely dressed as fine as him, wouldn't even think of churning butter, or even wonder where butter come from. I pondered how old was his wife when they married. Is she pretty? Is there a picture in their house of her with a baby on her lap?

"Delicious," he said. "So refreshing." He pulled out a big linen handkerchief and rubbed it across his mouth.

It pleased me to think I served the city fellow something he probably didn't have very often, something I take for granted. One good thing about having your own cow and chickens. You always know who's handled your milk and eggs.

I leaned forward with my forearms on the table. It was my turn to watch Winn McPherson as he picked up his brown briefcase and unbuckled it. Smooth and graceful like, he took out some papers. He begun to read and I could feel the power of having clothes and learning. His voice lost its neighborly tone, and I imagined him speaking in a courtroom. I fixed on the words, trying not to get lost in how he sounded or how he looked as he read my dead husband's will.

"I, Notice Hershall, Jr., bequeath all worldly assets, property, real and personal, including estate, stock and movables, and all proceeds of notes due, after any expenses, to wife Emmalene Hershall." Winn looked up. "That means he left you all the farm acreage, the stock, the buildings, and contents. There's an attachment here detailing the barn, chicken-house, toolshed…all his holdings."

I smiled a little thinking this gentleman was too refined to name the word "privy."

He read on: "…the equipment, stock, and household furniture." He looked up from his papers. "Mr. Hershall never borrowed money as he dealt only in cash. But you will have access to his good references if you ever have need of them."

My dead husband should have told me about everything if he was going to leave it in my care. But he hadn't. I didn't know if there was money in a bank or hid somewhere.

Of a sudden, I realized that no mention was made of any other heir. "What about Mr. Hershall's son, Big Jake, which is Jakie's daddy?"

"My father, Judge McPherson, was told fairly recently by Mr. Hershall that his son is deceased by his own hand."

I caught my breath. "I didn't know that." I put my hands to my cheeks and looked at the boy playing on the floor. Now his daddy would never come to see him.

The lawyer continued reading. "I leave the guardianship and well-being of my grandson, Jake Mickey Hershall, into the care of my wife, Emmalene Hershall, who is named sole executrix."

I had a odd feeling of softness for Mr. Hershall. All the time I thought he hated me and now to find out he trusted me with everything.

The lawyer laid a manicured hand on the table very near my arm. "It's fairly apparent that your husband wanted you to receive his entire estate with nothing for his deceased wife's relatives."

It saddened me to think Jakie had no parents, even if he didn't remember them. Now his granddaddy was gone, too.

"Emmalene? May I call you Emmalene?"

I glanced at his fingers laying on the table so close to my arm. He saw my look and moved his hand.

"Your husband dealt mostly with my father, Winston Senior. When the firm received confirmation that Mr. Hershall's son had died, Mr. Hershall, asked Father to update the will. He carefully worded it so there would be no mistake. You inherit everything and have sole custody of young Jake."

The lawyer leaned back and pulled at the edges of his bristly upper lip. "I think he appreciated how well you took care of the boy."

A question came to me. Had the Hershalls or the Fieldings in the mountains ever wanted Jakie? Since my step-father and Mr. Hershall's first wife was sister and brother—that made Jakie second cousin to my stepbrothers, Hack and Conrad. Mr. Hershall never mentioned any letters from them.

Winn McPherson turned to a different page. "Oh, yes," he said. "There's a recent acquisition of a few acres of bottomland property directly across Landing Run Creek, a cornfield I believe? The land was transferred to Mr. Hershall in April of this year. That belongs to you, too."

I sat straight up. Miz Annie's cornfield! Even if Mr. Hershall had bought it, I felt like it was still Annie's. Yet I felt some bit of pride at being the owner of it, being free to walk there, to sit in the middle of the land between the two families I knew best in Landing Run.

The lawyer brought a tortoise-shell writing pen from an inside pocket and explained that I should sign to accept the responsibility of executrix. After reading the pages, I signed my name where he pointed and looked up to see his eyes wide. What did he think? That I couldn't read or write? I had a flashback of my mother sitting with me ever night teaching me, helping me practice the letters of the alphabet and learn the multiplication tables.

The lawyer blew on the fresh ink, fanned the papers, then folded half of the sheets and handed them to me. He stuck the rest in his briefcase.

He stood to leave. "Emmalene?" It sounded like a question while he looked at me with raised eyebrows.

I pondered if it was okay for him to call me by my first name, then nodded.

"Your husband didn't mention any cash, though we have reason to think he may have some hidden away."

I kept a blank face as his meaning sunk in.

"I'm sure that if you locate said funds that have been illegally acquired, you'll of course inform us and we will consult the proper authorities."

I looked away hoping I wasn't coloring. Was there a smile lurking on his pretty lips? The sheriff had shot Mr. Hershall! Do they think I'll go running to them if I find the money they killed him over?

The lawyer gently stamped his foot to loosen the trousers that clung to his leg, outlining his calf, thick with muscle. He pulled at his knotted tie and his ring caught the sunlight from the window. He covered his mouth and gave a teeny cough, then fiddled with his mustache.

I worried what he was trying to say. Why did he stand there wrinkling his forehead? I glanced at Jakie who was tapping his fingers against the jar and making squeaky rabbit sounds. Was this fine gentleman going to tell me that I might could lose the boy? Was there a question that I wasn't worthy to take care of him? Pain flashed through my temples as I waited for the man to speak.

His lips curled up at the corners. I wished he'd hurry on up and get it over with. "Emmalene. I want to offer my condolences for the loss of your husband."

I'd been holding my breath, but now let it out.

"Of course, you know the case against Mr. Hershall's moonshine operation is still pending…"

"What do you mean, still pending?" I held my copies of the will so tight the edges crimped.

"Now, don't you worry. The question of Sheriff Winters and his culpability in the killing of your husband, I'm sure, will lead to a quiet settlement."

I breathed hard. My doubts about whether Mr. Hershall had took the first shot at the officers was all the time put up against my knowing how prideful he was. His way of speaking had been tough. "Anybody goes against me or mine will bleed! I've never backed down yet and I ain't commencing to."

The lawyer was still talking "…was known to be engaged in… ah…certain illegal activities, but as you are aware, the neighbors are closed-mouthed."

My face had frozen into a stare. Sweat prickled under my arms and my mouth was dry. What was he asking of me?

"As your representative, I think you should know this: The law has reason to think that Mr. Hershall had a man in his employ. Making the whiskey. Illegally." He coughed again, sniffed, and stretched his neck away from his collar. "If you know the whereabouts of said helper, you must come forward with the information."

Les! They want me to give his name. I hoped the man couldn't read my mind while it screamed. Les. Les.

I walked outside with the lawyer but couldn't find words.

He touched his hat, then untied his mare's reins. He smiled. "If you need ready cash to maintain your household or meet expenses, Judd, Smith and McPherson would be most happy to assist you in selling any properties you so designate."

I shaded my eyes with the papers I held and watched him climb into the saddle. A flying angle of wild geese honked overhead.

"I thank you for taking the time to ride all the way out here," I finally said.

"Oh, no trouble at all. I'm glad to do it."

He continued to sit in the saddle and look down at me til I spoke. "Well, good bye."

"I guess I'd best be on my way home. My wife will be expecting me."

The horse and rider rode down the lane of red and gold leaves and bounced out of sight.

It turned out ever body knew what all Winn McPherson had to say to me before I did. When Miz Annie asked me to come to her house and snap beans, she told me how. "That young lawyer's wife in Bardstown is a little snoop. She uses the same dressmaker as Retta and said in front of her that she got into her husband's satchel and read the old man's will. And then Retta told ever body at church."

Miz Annie and me were setting on her back porch with aprons full of string beans. Pulling off the heads and strings, the hollow popping made up for me not saying anything. For I could have just spit. My private business—and I was the last to know. And I could only guess what all lies was made up along with what was true.

Annie gave me time to say something, but I kept quiet and rummaged around in my apron to find any whole beans among the culls.

Finally, she talked about something else. "Well, I heard from Les last week, even though Boone told him not to write. Would you like me to read you his letter?"

I knew she was smoothing over if I was mad, and she was being nice so I nodded.

Miz Annie carried the letter in her apron. Reminded me of myself. She put it close to her eyes and read it straight through.

> October 13, 1910
> Dear Maw and all the family,
>   Thought I would drop you all a few lines to say this finds me fairly well and hope you are the same. Boone says my safety is not sure yet, so don't answer me back.

>You didn't let on much in your letter whether Emmalene is ok. Well I was glad to hear from you just the same and that Mr. Hershall had a nice burial. I sure hope you are doing all right with all the worry of the kids and all. I am sending this postal order, sure hope it helps out.
>
>Have been working on the farm here for Boone's Uncle Joe what owns many a acre. I like driving a team to plow same as driving a wagon to pick up late beans and squash and carry it to a farmers market. And as this last cold snap finished the rest of the crops here I need to find some other kind of job since I cant lay around and Uncle Joe says there is truck farming down south. They grow winter gardens same as summer. He says plenty money to be made in hauling oranges, grapefruits, dates, pecans. Sometimes I am still getting in the corn and I hear all the birds going south and turtledoves cooing distant like and I hear all this and it brings back old memories. I just stand and dream a while and I could just scream.

Miz Annie covered her eyes and I was about to cry myself. I stood up to say I better get Jakie and head on home, and she put her hand on my arm. "Emmalene, time here in Landing Run goes slow," she said, "and because ever day is like another, unusual things catch you up."

I saw in Miz Annie's troubled face, she had more to say.

"I hear tell that after Eliza Boone heard Old Man Hershall's mother, Patience, was a Catholic she thinks Jakie ought to be, too. And she is talking to Father Donnelly out at church to see if he could help her and Boone get custody so Jakie would have two Catholic parents."

I had to sit back down. I had told Miz Rice about the trunk I found upstairs and the old letter that had been returned to Patience Cutler Hershall. I never thought how many people Miz Rice would tell. I had been worried that Bertie would say I was unfit, but never thought about Eliza Boone bringing me this new trouble.

"Miz Annie, they can't have Jakie! His granddaddy said I have his charge and I got a lawyer to back me up!" I was shaking, but not scared. It was a nerve action hitting me and making me want to fight.

"If I was you, I'd go straight to Father Donnelly and let him know who you are. He is a old man, but he still knows right from wrong. And you can do good by getting him on your side."

"I can't believe Boone would do this to me," I said.

"It's not him, it's Eliza. Boone might not even know what she's up to. But corn harvesting comes pretty soon since we had the first good frost and the Boones has the biggest corn husking party you ever saw. Ever body will be there all day and night, and I wanted you to know."

The very next morning I got Jakie all dressed up and put on my rose-colored dress. I wrapped up the black mourning clothes and veil in a oil cloth parcel to give it back to Miz Rice. I did not want to buy it nor keep beholden to her, after her gossiping on what I told her about Patience's letter.

Besides, I didn't feel like a widow woman wearing black, same as I never felt married. And I didn't imagine being a mother but neither was I a unmarried girl without children. I couldn't tell what to feel but it was something different than before Mr. Hershall died.

As I drove the buggy out Landing Run Road, I heard cows mooing in a way that said, "Come milk me, for my bag is full and if you don't hurry, I'll go to bawling." With big families most all had a cow, maybe two.

Jakie listened and watched ever thing, too, and made joyful noises when he heard dogs yipping or if a squirrel or a possum ran across in front of us.

We passed a catalpa tree that reminded me of the giant at Miz Annie's. Her tree stands twice as tall as her house, and its bare limbs has the look of a sick old woman losing flesh. Partly in the sun and partly in the shade makes the ridged bark look painted in two gray colors. I imagine the young tree seeds were carried out here to the road by boys like Les and Dolin playing like they was smoking. Miz Annie said yesterday, "In the fall, those two used to pretend the catalpa pods were cigars." She guessed that's how they learned to smoke.

Thinking about Les was a pastime of mine. My ears always perked up when anything was said, like yesterday when Garr come in and sat down on the porch while we snapped beans. "Now, Old Darlin," he said to Annie, and he had put his hand down heavy on the rocker arm. "I wouldn't worry just yet. Les is right to keep hid for now. Boone said somebody over to the courthouse heard about that Sheriff Winters building a case about who shot first."

"Les wasn't even there," said Miz Annie.

"I know. But out of the four men raiding the place, one sides with Winters saying that Old Man Hershall shot first, and the others says Winters killed the old man before he even aimed his rifle."

Annie shivered. "So they need to make it okay for the law's part by catching Les?"

"That's the way Boone's friend tells it. Don't fret. Even if somebody turned in Les's name, they didn't see him on the shine. They can't pin anything on him. After the hearing is settled, he'll come home. You'll see."

Garr meant to ease his wife, but I was hanging on to his words, too. Garr being Les's daddy told me he was talking brave for Annie, but still he made sense. He must think that old Judge McPherson would lean to the side of the people, not the outsider, Winters.

Seeing his maw and papa together made me think of Les even more strong and think ahead if he would be like Garr in his older years. Miz Annie had said that when they first married, Garr could plow all day and fiddle all night.

When I got to Jackson Highway I went straight to Rice's Store. I could tell Miz Rice must of felt guilty over gossiping about me, for first thing, she went to explaining. "Oh, Emmalene, I swear I had no idea what Eliza Boone was up to when I told her about you finding that old letter! Eliza was a Cutler before she married, so I just thought she'd like to know that one of her long ago women-folks had left some writing to tell about her marrying that boy from the mountains and how he was Old Man Hershall's father and all."

I didn't want to pretend like it was all right, but I remembered how Miz Rice had been one of the few women speaking to me up until the old man's death. Besides, she had practically set me up in business by selling me her hens.

I gave her a little smile. "Well, Miz Rice, it weren't no secret, really. You couldn't know that Eliza meant to take Jakie away from me."

Maybe I was aiming my words to punish Miz Rice for talking loose. But when her mouth dropped open and her eyes looked guilty, I touched her arm. "It's okay. Eliza's not going to get Jakie for it's all written down legal that I have his charge."

"Oh, it's good to see your dimples, again," Miz Rice said with a sigh.

I handed her the black mourning dress she had leant me for the funeral.

"You didn't have to bring this back. It's yours, a present from me and Mr. Rice."

I just shook my head. "Have you brought any letters in for me?"

Miz Rice turned to the slots behind her where they put mail that wasn't picked up for a couple of days from the outside boxes. "You've got several pieces here."

I said my goodbyes and led Jakie out to the buggy, sure that Miz Rice had done all but steam open my letters to read them.

When I got settled behind the reins, I looked through the small stack looking for something from Les, although I told myself that there would be nothing.

It was all business mail addressed to Mrs. Notice Hershall, Jr. The name didn't suit me, yet I was proud at being the new owner of the farm and valuable timbered woods. I liked being known as the head of the house now that Mr. Hershall was dead.

He had never let me see any mail, so it satisfied me to hold the long white envelopes with return addresses of streets from downtown Bardstown. The mortician had sent a statement listing all items for Mr. Hershall's funeral, stamped "Paid in Full." I figured Boone must of got his money back when he sold the hidden whiskey. I appreciated Boone's kindness, but worried about his good deeds until I knew for sure what he planned to do about getting Jakie. All his niceness wouldn't make up for trying to take the boy away from me.

There was a personal note with the mortician's statement of accounts. "If you should again require our services, we would consider it our sacred duty to assist you in your time of need."

The bank president had mailed me a typed letter. "Mrs. Hershall, We will be most happy to administer your accounts, as we have done in the past for Mr. Notice Hershall, Jr. Very Respectfully Yours…"

Winston Judd McPherson, Jr., had also added a personal note to his law firm's request that I continue doing business with their office. He signed it, "I am, Very Truly Yours."

I vowed to answer all the letters and set up business in my own name. If there was any cash money coming in, I wanted the banker to put it in a new account for Emmalene Hershall. The first thing I would buy would be a dresser like the one Mother had. Hers was walnut, had three sets of drawers with brass pulls and a winged three-way mirror.

In the middle of Mother's dresser, she had placed a wood box with slots to keep receipts, writing paper and mailing envelopes. I would buy one for myself, just like hers. Now that I was getting letters, I wanted a nice place to keep them.

It was a short ride from Rice's Store to Our Lady of Hope Church. Jakie was sleepy but I feared to take him home and lose the courage I built from getting straight with Miz Rice and receiving mail in my name.

The trees along the road still had a few leaves on mostly bare limbs. A slanting autumn sun shined golden brown on corn shocks, blue in the sky and gray on the fence posts.

I saw the church building was small but nice built—not brick, but split poplar logs sealed up tight against winter rains and snow. At the right hand side of the church was a graveyard, a plot bigger than the churchyard, set back a piece from Jackson Highway. In the back and between the church and the graves was small rooms for the priest's house. A stand of pines on the hillside beyond made a sweeping half circle, protecting the church property and headstones. Nobody left out in the cold.

I knocked soft at first, then loud. While I waited for a answer, I watch six shiny crows perched on the rail fence this side of the graveyard. Their feathers was so black they seemed to change to darkest blue and purple while I took their measure. The birds set fairly near together and looked to be almost twenty inches long apiece. Much bigger up close than I had ever noticed. They did not flap their wings nor fly away when I lifted my arm to knock. Just sat and glared at me with sharp eyes on each side of their heads. They made me feel like I was unwelcome and this was their place. I calculated they was looking to see whose corn they could get into, but first they would get shed of me.

Father Donnelly, looking like a chubby old angel with pink cheeks, pink scalp and round belly, finally answered the door. I introduced myself and asked if I could bring in Jakie.

The priest didn't understand at first that Jakie was asleep and I didn't want to leave him in the buggy. Does he think I'm leaving the boy on his doorstep?

He finally figured what I was saying, and I laid Jakie on the parlor sofa and covered him with my shawl.

I sat down in front of the fireplace where the priest pointed out a chair, and he took a long time arranging his long black garment and running his fingers around his starched white collar. Then he held his hands in his lap and pressed each thumb and forefinger together. He seemed uneasy. The dancing fire lit up his soft cheeks and fine white hair.

It's me should be edgy. Here I am a non-Catholic, not having spoken to a priest before. And I was also nervous not knowing what Eliza or Bertie might have said I did with Albert. I was satisfied this man had already heard true and untrue things about me.

The priest uncrossed and recrossed his legs. Finally he looked straight at me. "So I understand you are keeping company with young Dolin Linkahan."

I was about knocked out of my chair. "Uh…no…what?"

Father Donnelly sat there fiddling with his black robes and I couldn't help but think he was wearing a dress. If it wasn't for those black shoes and black pants legs sticking out at the bottom, he'd look like a little old man dressed up like a woman.

His voice rang back to me, "I have been concerned about him keeping company with a non-Catholic and I'm glad you came to see me."

Father? Should I call him Father? I spoke up. "Father Donnelly, I am not talking to Dolin Linkahan. I am a widow for five weeks now. I have the care of Jakie Hershall, and I've come to talk to you about one in your church that may be trying to take him from me."

The priest fluttered again. He coughed and studied the fire. Then he bunched the tips of his fingers together. "I thought you had come to ask about taking instructions to become a Catholic in preparation for marrying Dolin Linkahan. I am not aware of anyone trying to take the boy from you."

So many ideas rushed through my mind. First, I needn't worry that Eliza had talked to Father—unless he had just plain forgot. I'd heard Miz Rice say that the old priest was somewhat dotty, sometimes not knowing on a Sunday that it was time to say Mass. Early church goers might find him sitting outside in his chair when they drove up in their buggies. He was too old for the bishop to transfer out to another parish, so they built him a little home and let him stay at Our Lady of Hope.

If Eliza had come asking if she could get Jakie, I set down that trouble to take in the other possibility. What if I did want to become a Catholic? It seemed like Father was okay with that. It sure would make my life easier in Landing Run and I didn't really have a loyalty to any other church. I figured God was personal, not outside of you or in a place you had to go to and worship. Mother never went to any church and she was the best person I ever heard of.

Father was saying something about "the right reasons." I wondered what the wrong reasons would be. If a person wanted to fit in with the neighbors, go to their church, believe what they did—weren't those good reasons? Maybe he was thinking I had too many sins, too big of sins to forgive. I remembered Miz Annie talking about the rules of going to church on Sundays and what she called a Holy Day of Obligation.

Miz Annie had said, "All Saint's Day is coming up November first. That means all Catholics must attend Mass same as Sundays under pain of mortal sin."

"What's mortal sin?"

"Well, there's three things make something a mortal sin. It must be big, you must know it is big, and you must want to do it."

"And what happens to you if you do it?"

"If you die without making a good confession, you will go straight to hell."

Miz Annie had sounded delighted with the rules. For every answer I got I had more questions. Like what all is a big sin and what exactly do the Catholics believe hell is and what is a good confession? Is there such of a thing as a bad confession? And if you never heard of a Holy Day of Obligation, then does it mean you never sinned even though you missed Mass all your life?

I watched the priest tapping his fingertips together, looking at me. Was he waiting for a answer?

I blurted out, "I want to feel like I belong here!"

"So it's not just because of Dolin being Catholic? You must know that Holy Mother Church frowns on mixed marriages."

"Marriage? I'm not thinking about that any time soon!" I meditated on who was spreading all the rumors. Well, I guess everybody is. People like to hear things and they like to tell things. Who's talking to who is always a good story.

The little priest shifted in his chair. "Well, now. Nobody says you're getting married. It's just that courtship is a serious thing. You must keep yourself pure as the newly driven snow, and you should never set out with anyone you would not or could not marry."

My voice sounded loud in my own ears. "I just want to take care of Jakie, and if I go to church I'll be like everybody else."

"So you are willing to baptize Jakie too?"

"Well, he doesn't know much about religion and all that, but I guess I would."

Mr. Hershall's face appeared to me. He probably would come back and haunt me forever for saying such a thing. Make his grandson a Catholic? He would be so mad he'd be spitting instead of talking.

Father Donnelly put three fingers against his cheek. "Come to think of it, Eliza Boone—who was born a Cutler—came to look at the old 1800s Baptismal Records and found that Notice Hershall, Jr.—your dead husband—was baptized the day he was born by the midwife who delivered him."

He frowned. "Of course, you know we could not give him a Catholic burial because he was not in his church."

I expected him to wag his finger at me, and I wanted to say that the old man had not asked so it wasn't much a concern to him. But I held my thoughts and let the little priest go on.

"By rights one can see that had Patience Cutler, Mr. Hershall's mother, lived, you would have married into a Catholic family." His face lit up from the firelight and even brighter from a light inside him. "Young Jakie, yonder, would automatically have already been baptized." His face was complete smiles.

My feelings rode up and down like a train on a mountain track.

Whether Mr. Hershall believed or not, he was recorded as baptized. Any way, he couldn't judge me for how I took care of Jakie now. For the priest seemed to be saying I might could easy be a Catholic, especially if I got Jakie baptized too. Besides, just talking about it didn't make it true. If I changed my mind and didn't like all these rules, I would just back out. I will say I want to find out about the church, and I'll take Jakie ever Sunday, and the Father and Eliza and anybody else will see that I really want to be a good person and a fit mother.

The priest stood up to say goodbye. "Emmalene, I'm going to give this copy of The Baltimore Catechism to you. Look at it and read the first twenty questions."

I took the book and felt I was holding all the answers to my future. I would read as much as I could beyond that. Didn't Father say there were over one thousand four hundred questions? I needed to read more. I would look up All Saints Day, a Holy Day of Obligation, because that was coming up in a few days.

Emmalene
November 1910

November first was All Saints' Day and I drove my buggy to Miz Annie's house to ride to church with the Richmans. Annie had told me, "I am walking into Our Lady of Hope Church with Jakie and you, your first visit!"

Now that Les was gone, the oldest boy at home was Foster and he gave his hand to help his mother into the front seat of the wagon. Christina and Nan Mary settled the little ones in the clean straw in the back.

"When we get there, you hold your head up," said Annie. "You are dressed so pretty in your rose-colored dress, and you have as much right as any to be there."

I felt my face flush remembering that I was wearing this same dress when Albert said the color suited me like red on a apple. "And they won't think I'm an outsider who doesn't belong?" I asked.

Miz Annie drew her shoulders up. "Ever body knows you done went to see Father Donnelly and he gave you the catechism book."

Then Annie mentioned a invitation that made me smile. "Boone said to make sure you and Jakie come to the corn husking at his place. It'll be in a couple of weeks, after his corn is all got in."

As the wagon rolled past her yard, Annie named the fall-blooming flowers…purple asters, goldenrod, and orange berries on the bitter sweet vines. A sudden squall had come early that morning and the dirt in the garden was just wetted enough to smell earthy like it was letting out secrets.

Foster drove the wagon slow, aiming to miss potholes. Christina held Jakie while Nan Mary held their two-year-old brother, Nace. They played a singsong game where Christina touched Nace's head with one finger. "Here is where the cat sat." Then she bounced her finger to his forehead, "Here is where the cat jumped to!" She put a finger directly under each of his eyes saying, "Oh, I found me some eye-peepers!" and "What a nose-smeller!"

I glanced at Christina several times, knowing pretty well from the way she had stood and watched me and Dolin the day of Mr. Hershall's funeral, she was sweet on Dolin. I wanted to tell her that him and me had a respect and liking for each other, and if she heard anything more, it was gossip. I didn't want to say, "I favor your big brother, Les," for I had no right to announce this feeling. Especially me being a new widow and just now going to the church for the first time.

The wagon rolled into the churchyard, and the family climbed down. I studied Miz Annie and her girls, how they straightened their hats and arranged their skirts. They kept their voices low while they greeted friends, for all was about to enter God's home.

Bertie Linkahan stood at the front pew guiding her boys in, hissing under her breath, "Go on clear to the end. Cleophus, grab him!" She frowned as one redhead slipped out the other side like a bull out of a chute, and ran toward the back of the church. Bertie's pocketbook rocked back and forth on one arm while her youngest baby lolled his head against her. Nine boys! How did she get them all in clean shirts and overalls?

I looked for Dolin and saw him leaning on his cane in the back of church.

I thought of what Les had said he told Dolin when they was growing up. Les didn't think much of him talking Latin, dressing up in wide-sleeve white shirts to be a altar boy. Les said to me, "A person don't have to put on a show to believe in God."

I kind of felt like Les. So why am I here and wanting to please my neighbors so much? But I had to admit, it was a nice feeling to be inside this place because it felt holy.

Looking toward the altar, I saw Father Donnelly in his white satin robes and standing with his back to all us in church. The Richmans and me sat back far enough I might could see people I knew. Older men half-sat on the polished pews, most kneeled on the padded kneelers. Mothers held babies, some sleeping, some jabbering, some sucking on a sugar tit.

The Catholics seemed at ease hearing the Latin words, but I couldn't help believing they were getting lost in their own heads. I couldn't tell by looking. The strangeness and mystery gave me pause, and didn't quite set right with me. It might be too different for me to become one of them.

All the women wore hats. Miz Annie had told me to wear a scarf and I had asked her, "Why do women have to wear hats in church?"

"A woman's hair is her pride," she said. "It ought to be covered so as not to distract others."

This did not make sense, for there was Retta, cocking her head this way and that and making the white ostrich plume flutter. She looked more like showing off her hat, not covering her hair. I had a thought of buying myself a hat as pretty as Retta's.

Father Donnelly's sermon was in English and about those in heaven, whether canonized or not. Annie whispered, "Canonized means made a saint by church law."

I had many things to learn.

Annie had told me this was a high Mass. "That means they sing the parts that's only spoke in a low Mass."

There wasn't any church organ and I could hear Christina's clear voice where she stood with other girls in the choir to one side of Father. His voice was trembly and the girls did most of the singing in Latin. I know these girls don't know what they're singing.

Maribelle Meadors stood slightly behind Nan Mary. Maribelle had swept her hair back from her face yet her blonde curls twisted out of her pink bonnet—a bit of pink lace and dangling ribbons. She puffed out her bottom lip to blow a strand of hair from her mouth, and I saw why Les might be wanting her.

When Mass was over, people walked outside smiling and talking and patting each other on the back. They have done their duty and now can go about their business knowing they are righteous. I felt righteous too.

Riding home from church, Christina and Nan Mary sang "Holy God, We Praise Thy Name" to the kids while me and Miz Annie talked. She told me about Bertie one time being a stranger in Landing Run herself. "Bertie was eighteen living with her family in Owensboro when she got swept off her feet by Wyman Linkahan. They upped and married, and he brought her back here to his home place, and they commenced to have nine babies, all boys." Although, after Dolin, she lost three babies before their time, she made up for it with having the others so close together.

Annie told me Bertie's last one was born in March, a week before I got here. "Her husband, Wyman, was a rounder. Drank more than enough and took off for weeks at a time on his horse-trading deals."

Annie looked at me like she questioned if I was listening, and then she told more. "Now, his older brother, James Linkahan, is different. He left Landing Run as a young man and set up a furniture-making business in Owensboro. Not rich, but plenty well off. His wife died about a year ago."

"Miz Rice told me Bertie's husband died from the kick of a young horse," I said.

"A fitting end. The horse was too wild to break and it broke Wyman."

I thought about Bertie having so many children and no husband to help. "I reckon that's why she hovers over Dolin so close and acts like she hates me. Maybe she figgers I'd try to get him away from her."

Even if I pitied Bertie as a widow woman, I also liked knowing something personal about her. Something more than her setting ever body against me. I wanted Miz Annie to know the truth about what happened with Albert.

"Miz Annie, I got to tell you. You remember the day Halley's Comet come through and ever body joined up at Rice's for a celebration and the Moonlight Dance? Well, I wasn't there. I was home."

Miz Annie looked at me, her eyebrows wrinkled together.

"I rode in the wagon with Albert Nobles to Boone's little tenant cabin—the one across the road and down the lane from Boone's house? But I only wanted a drink of water. And when I figured what Albert was going to ask of me, I hurried on back home, and nothing else happened, and I know Bertie has told something bad to ever body."

I was amazed when Miz Annie threw her head back and laughed. "Girl, have you worried over that? Well, Bertie never told anybody but me, and she ain't gonna ever tell no body else what happened."

I stared with my mouth open.

"Wyman will be dead a year come Christmas, and Bertie has been writing to his brother, James in Owensboro. James come to town to visit her and they was in that cabin together when they heard Albert's wagon pull up."

I breathed so hard I was getting a headache.

"Bertie tells me everything. She said James had tied the horse in the woods behind them, but they only had time to grab their coats and the baby in his covers and run out the back door to hide against the cabin wall."

"You mean Bertie never talked about seeing me?"

"She thought you seen them from the kitchen window—or heard them outside laughing—and worried you were going to tell about her."

"Then why is she so mean to me?"

"A rat smells its own hole."

By the time Jakie and me got back home, I was mad. If Bertie is carrying on with her brother-in-law, then she needn't act so holy with me! I had been studying immorality and sinning between single people, which wasn't thought any less wrong than sinning with one who is married. But it didn't seem equal to me. And not as wrong for either kind of sin, knowing how needy a person can get.

I thought about how lonesome, how despairing Bertie must be—enough to risk getting caught with a man. I made up my mind I would say something nice to her at Boone's corn husking. In my heart, I knew it was for me to feel better, not her.

A couple weeks after All Saint's Day, I drove the buggy to Rice's Store. I settled Jakie in a chair not too close to the stove and gave him his favorite stick to tap on a can. When there wasn't a lot of customers, I whispered to Miz Rice. "Out in my shed is three fifty-pound bags of sugar, a few thirty-gallon jugs, some copper plate and a new fifty-gallon barrel that I ain't got use for. I wonder if you would take them back and give me credit?"

Miz Rice looked left, then right and whispered, "Oh, I reckon that special order Mr. Hershall bought off us never did get used." She lowered her voice even more. "Emmalene, that stuff is too heavy for you to lift. Let's think on how to get it loaded up at your place and back here during the night when nobody is around." She nodded and sucked on her teeth.

A couple of days later, me and Jakie walked out our lane a piece to a spot where I'd seen wild mint growing. The chilly days made me want hot mint tea in front of the fireplace.

We headed home, and in the lane in front of us I saw Dolin on horseback. He sat easy in the saddle, waiting til we got to him. "I was just coming to see you," he said.

Walking slow to my kitchen door, my thoughts flitted this way and that and my stomach was taking a nervous turn. Was he about to declare feelings that I didn't have for him? I had got used to telling ever body that things weren't like that between us.

Dolin got off his horse and limped behind me. While I set Jakie at the table, Dolin grinned. "Nobody knows outside family, but me and Christina are getting hitched on Christmas Day right after Midnight Mass." The bleached skin around his burned eyebrow pulled into laugh wrinkles.

I took a deep breath and said a little too loud, "Oh, Dolin, that's good! I didn't know you all was talking to each other."

He stretched out his legs and pain went across his face. It took me back to when he was so bad burned.

When the pain left, Dolin's face turned happy. "I knew Christina all my life," he said, "but seems like the past couple of months she grew up. All the sudden, we both knew we was gonna get married. Father Donnelly will announce the first banns on December fourth."

I had read about the banns in my catechism. For three weeks in a row, right before his sermon, the priest would announce the names of the two engaged, and say, "If any of you know cause why these persons should not be joined together in Holy Matrimony, you are to declare it." Miz Annie had told me it was mostly to keep first cousins from marrying.

Dolin said he didn't know where they would set up housekeeping, but probably would start out with the Richmans. "Here's something else I'm not supposed to tell, but I'm gonna tell you. I think Maw is going to marry Uncle James." He looked pleased. "And if they move somewhere else, then maybe Christina and me can move into the home place."

It was like Miz Annie said: "You think nothing much happens and all the sudden, somebody is born, somebody dies, or somebody is married." I doubted Christina would like it if her mother-in-law to-be got married about the same time as her. And Bertie had a young baby; what if she got in the family way again, right when Christina did?

It eased me somewhat to think that soon the gossip would stop about Dolin and me. Dolin is a good match for Christina, four years older and both of them Catholic and lifelong neighbors.

Dolin shook his head. "I sure wish we could write to Les—I know he'll be proud to be my brother-in-law."

He stood to leave and I had a idea. "Dolin, do you think you and Cleophus and maybe Jimmy Lee might could bring your farm wagon and haul some things back to Rices? Things Mr. Hershall bought and I don't need?"

"Boone's hired men has brought in his field corn and the husking party starts tomorrow morning, early," he said. "So what if we bring the wagon and take that stuff to the store, sometime after that?"

The early morning sky had no sun, but light enough I could see straw-colored grass under the frost. I got Jakie dressed in good warm clothes for we'd be all day; Miz Annie said Boone's corn husking was the biggest in Landing Run and we'd still be there til way up in the night.

Jakie sat on the buggy seat beside me, bundled so tight in lap robes, he couldn't stir. Only bobbed his head up and down the same time the horse did.

Once on the Boone property, the first building was their biggest barn. Corn stubble—dry stalks and stobs tied to poles—dotted the far fields. Winter-feed for Boone's farm animals.

Pigs was held in stout wood-rail fences made in a zigzag pattern but laid in straight-boxed pens. The closer we got, the more Jakie squealed.

Some days I'd be walking past Boone's and see pigs running wild in his woods beyond, feeding on mast—hard-shelled acorns and nuts. But now his hogs snorted and grunted at the slop troughs, not knowing that freezing days had come and soon they'd get butchered. They's resting up, getting fat on corn and don't have an idee it's to sweeten their meat before the slaughter.

Jakie had wriggled loose from his wraps and pointed at the pigs, wanting to jump down from the wagon. I held on to him and clucked the horse into a ambling gait, guiding the buggy around to where I saw Boone raking straw in a small pen. I got a whiff of sour smells from the feed troughs.

Boone waved. "Hey, Emmalene. I got to get two of my brood sows fastened up in here before all the little kids come round. Them mother pigs is mean when it comes to somebody touching one of their piggies. If it squeals, she'll attack. And bite!"

I had aimed to be there early, but already they was horseback riders and wagonloads of families spilling out. I stopped my buggy next to those lining up in a row between the farm buildings and the house. Most ever household owned a team of work horses or mules, so they was a lot of them, tied loose so they could chew grass. At least one was always sure to be lifting its tail, spreading its back haunches and relieving itself.

Jakie made excited noises seeing the kids who were let loose and running about the farmyards. Their parents was dressed in old clothes—the men in hats, overalls and flannel shirts and the women in dust caps and ever-day dresses, ready to shuck corn and have fun all the same time. Next few days they'd turn up at another farmer's house and do the same thing. I doubted anybody would offer to get in the corn Mr. Hershall had planted. I myself hadn't even looked at it since he died.

Cleophus and Jimmy Lee ran up to me and Jakie. Cleophus beamed. "Emmalene! Jimmy Lee and me got a big old pig cooking! We been up all night smearing it with sauce!" He pointed to smoke coming from a pine grove beside the back garden. A group of boys stood looking down into a dug pit.

I wanted to go inside the house, but the Richmans weren't there yet and I didn't have nerve enough to walk into Eliza's kitchen without Annie. I watched Cleophus working, whistling and fairly dancing while setting wooden benches around a mountain of piled corn, just outside the crib house.

When the Richmans drove their wagon in, Cleophus and Les's brother, Foster, took Jakie. I knew they wouldn't let him get hurt in the roughhousing. "Watch out he don't wander off," I said.

Christina jumped from the Richman wagon ahead of her mother, Miz Annie. I wanted to say something to Christina about her getting married, but thought I better wait til I was sure ever body else knew about it. The Richmans was all friendly, but nobody mentioned a wedding.

Christina smiled and stood back to let me walk into the pantry that led into the kitchen. My heart beat faster—I didn't like feeling scared of Eliza.

The room had a low ceiling with strings of dried mulberries, hot peppers, and shuck beans along with cloth sacks of dried sweet potatoes, apples and peaches hanging from the overhead beams. Stacked along the side wall was baskets of crook-necked squash and red onions.

I was disbelieving of all I beheld. Miz Annie laughed. "I couldn't wait to see your face looking at what all Eliza puts up. And this is just the first!"

We walked past a plank stand of pumpkins, some with small stems still on them. A bushel of hulled walnuts sat in a dark corner, and on a deep, heavy shelf above it was a gallon of honey and two jugs of sorghum molasses. "Eliza feeds a lot of people in Landing Run who don't have much. But don't let on you know—she and Boone does it secret."

In the kitchen, Eliza stood at a counter with an iron water pump beside the sink. Hardly nobody had water in their kitchen, and I thought how lucky she was to have a man willing and handy enough to fix it so she didn't have to draw well water or go to the springhouse or the creek.

Eliza was rolling dough and dipping flour from a large barrel for to make cobblers, while hot blackberry and peach fillings bubbled on the stove.

Her thin face was red as she flung orders to the young girls who stood around. "Get me that black iron skillet." She was loud for such a small woman. "Christina, I'm glad you're here. You can set in to peeling potatoes—we'll need a right smart."

Eliza barely looked at me and Miz Annie, but she called over her shoulder to Retta, "Why don't you mix up some cinnamon, nutmeg, and cloves and boil them in a little sugar water for the spiced blueberries?"

"Can we help?" asked Miz Annie. "Might we go down to the cellar and bring up anything?"

Eliza looked up, eyes and lips hard. "Well, I guess if you don't mind, you can get some apples and make brown-betty or strudel. And whatever else you see we'll want."

She hadn't said a word to me and looked down again at her big mixing bowl.

I followed Miz Annie outside where the smells of pork roasting in the pit was good and strong and mouth-watering. Slanted double doors led to the underground cellar.

Miz Annie felt her way down, her feet measuring each plank step and her hands gripping beams at the sides. Behind her I said, "It's plain Eliza don't want me here. I think I ought to go home."

"Don't you worry about her. She has the temper of a wet hen most all time anyway. Boone told me to invite you here."

"Maybe Boone asking me and Miz Eliza is two different things."

"Let me tell you. If you had not come she'd also have something to say about that. Probably say you're too good to help. A person just has to do whatever they want around her. You gonna catch heck any which way you go."

My eyes got used to the darkness, and I gazed at row after row of quart jars with glass lids and metal clamps to hold them on. The jars shined with colors: red tomatoes and tomato juice and tomato ketchup; and on a different shelf, green beans, yellow wax beans, butter beans, and lima beans. "My word! I never seed the like of canning! Eliza must work all day, ever day."

"She does that and she hires girls to help, too. "They's all kinds of food—preserved, canned, pickled, dried. And root vegetables is buried under straw in the garden.

Annie pointed for me to get the apples and tied up the ends of her apron to carry cabbage heads and parsnips. She nodded toward a far corner. "Look at that cabinet. Filled with fruitcakes she gives out at Christmas."

I remembered my mother making a heavy cake with dried fruit and aging it in whiskey-soaked towels.

Annie turned to go back upstairs. "Ever month or so Eliza brings a big mess of meat and stuff to my house and Bertie's house, says can we take it off her hands. She says she'd feel better knowing it didn't go to waste. She gives to Father Donnelly and I don't know who all."

My thoughts went one way then another. Here Eliza wanted to take Jakie away from me, yet she was so giving to others. I couldn't understand.

I wondered if the apples I carried in my apron might have come from Albert Nobles's orchard. I couldn't help blaming him for getting me to that cabin so's ever body thought we were carrying on.

When we got up from the cellar, it was mostly men sitting on the benches pulling shucks off the dried corn. Boone pointed out certain baskets. "Save the best ears for next spring's planting, and put all the stalks and leaves in the older baskets for to put in the barn for feeding. Nothing goes to waste."

It was a awful big crop, must have been two hundred or more bushels. When the baskets got full of shucked corn, the younger boys poured it in gunny sacks and hung them in the corncrib to finish drying out. They put baskets of nubbins, the short, ungrowed ears, in a closed-off bin in the pig shed.

I stood a minute, looking around the farm. Boone's log corncrib was bigger than most houses, setting up off the ground, built wide at the top, more narrow at the bottom with slatted sides where air could go through.

Besides the corncrib, he had a horse barn, a hay barn, a meat house, a hen house, a privy and a couple other out buildings. No wonder he and Eliza worked all time and had tenant farmers, too, that work for a dollar a day.

Eliza's kitchen had got crowded while Annie and me was in the cellar. Good! She won't notice me so much.

Women who had come for Mr. Hershall's wake and funeral, the same ones I saw when I went to Mass, looked easier with sweaty faces and cotton dust caps than in Sunday clothes. Even Retta had on a ever-day dress. She spoke to me while lifting the top off the green beans and ham to see if it needed some water.

Bertie had her hair in braids and a cap perched on top of her head. She stuffed half a rolled pancake, dripping with jam, into her mouth. "Gotta get rid of these stomach rumblings," she said, smiling. I thought her face changed when she saw it was me beside her.

Why do I even care what she and Eliza think? Miz Annie likes me and there's others that do. At least they speak to me, even if it's just to nod their heads.

Bertie swallowed a drink of coffee, then opened her mouth to cool her tongue. She tossed her head. "James wrote me yesterday. Said to look for him any day now. I just can't wait to see him and what all he brings for the boys."

I wished I could be happy like Bertie, speak easy as she did in front of all the women. As it was, I busied myself scraping carrots and peeling onions and keeping quiet.

Eliza looked around. "This kitchen is getting too crowded. Go on all you young girls out there and help the men shuck. You're just standing around in here getting in the way."

A pregnant woman beside the door started to leave but Miz Annie pulled her back. "Not you. You set down and rest."

"You go too, Maribelle," said Retta.

"Do I have to, Mama? I'll get my hands all roughed up and tear my fingernails."

"Go on, Sweetest One. Get your Papa's gloves and be careful of your dress. It's not exactly old enough to be wearing while you're doing farm work."

By mid-afternoon Boone called for a break. "Ever body wash up and take a smoke. I'll see if the old lady has got the dinner ready."

The workers filled a long table set in the great kitchen, and some sat on the porch. A smaller table was in the pantry. Tender, fresh pork had been carved into thick slabs and chunks and three women carried large platters around to dish it out. A line of serving bowls made its way from hand to hand: never-ending plates of hot biscuits, mounds of mashed potatoes with sliding roofs of butter, thick corn pudding, green peas cooked with onions and carrots, and baked sweet potatoes. One platter of fried chicken followed another.

Women refilled glasses of iced tea and milk, poured extra gravy, and served children sitting at the smaller table where I sat feeding Jakie.

Near dark, when Boone lit the lanterns, work was going at high speed. He brought homemade blackberry wine from the cellar and apple juice for the kids. More than one jug of whiskey came out of hiding and the men didn't even try to keep their swallows a secret.

I felt like I could shuck corn in my sleep—grab a ear, pull down the husk, twist and break off the stem pulling dried leaves and silks with it. Pitch the fodder one way and the shucked ear the other, then grab another.

The circle of workers grew more crowded as the women came out from cleaning the kitchen to help finish the husking. The mood got a little feisty with the kids asleep on pallets in the house. These Catholics seemed more spirited, almost rowdy, filled with a good dinner, their bodies close in the lantern-lit night.

My eye caught sight of two people near me whose hands grabbed the same ear of corn. A shout went up from the crowd as Dolin held up a red ear, which meant he got to kiss the girl of his choice. One young woman pointed at me. "Dolin gets to kiss Emmalene!"

The others took it up. "Kiss Emmalene! Kiss Emmalene!"

I shook my head and shrunk back, but the teasing kept on: "Here's Emmalene. What are you waiting for?"

I recognized Bertie's laughing voice. "I bet she's found a red corn ear before."

That stung me but I didn't say what I was thinking. Old biddy. She'd probably say she's just kidding. That's what a lot of people claim right after they hurt somebody's feelings.

I didn't aim to look at Dolin, but being close by I saw his face darken as he ducked his head.

Soon the crowd forgot the red corn ear and carried on with a different foolishness. In a little while I remembered whose other hand had reached for the red ear. Christina's. I looked around but she had stole away.

When I could leave the circle without being noticed, I walked out across the moonlit barnyard. The deep quiet seemed strange away from the laughing workers.

I pulled my wool shawl close around my shoulders and wandered toward the far side of the barn. No one there. Christina must've gone to the kitchen.

As I walked through the dark pantry to the kitchen door, I heard Eliza saying, "I baptize thee in the Name of the Father, and of the Son, and of the Holy Ghost. Amen."

Eliza was alone with Jakie. She stood over the worktable beside the sink and water pump. She had laid Jakie on his back and held his head in one hand and a cup of water in the other.

I ran up and pushed Eliza away and grabbed Jakie. Water dripped down his face and the back of his head, but he smiled and nodded up and down, up and down.

"What are you doing?" I heard myself screaming at Eliza. "I can't believe even you would go behind my back and do this!" I held Jakie tight. "How dare you take over and do for Jakie what is my privilege to decide!"

Eliza shrunk back and her voice squeaked. "I was afraid the little feller would die, and without baptism he'd go to limbo and never see the face of God. It was for his own good."

"No it wasn't! You have made it plain how much you hate me, and you took your chance to put this over on me!"

Eliza lifted her head and her voice got strong. "Well, I guess you might as well know. Jakie is not your blood kin and you can't call him yours. I've got a providing husband and a good home and I'm the one what should have him."

I didn't feel like it was me, raging. "I have took care of him like a mother, and his own grandfather left him in my charge. As anybody can see, you're mean and a sneak and you're the one that's not fit to have him!"

I yanked a towel from the sink and wiped off Jakie's head and whirled him toward the door. I stopped when Boone walked in. His face sagged as he stood looking down at the floor behind me. I turned half-way and saw Eliza sunk on her knees with her hands over her face.

Boone stepped aside as I rushed past him.

By the time I got Jakie in the buggy, I was crying. It looked like things were getting worse. Maybe becoming a Catholic would not help at all. Maybe things would go back to how it was when I came to Landing Run. No friends, and now no husband, even one as distant as Mr. Hershall.

I thought of Les hanging his hat on the nail inside my kitchen door. I could see his face still wet from scrubbing at the rain barrel before sitting down to supper when he finished a day working with Mr. Hershall. I wished I could see him push back his chair after eating and hear him say, "That was mighty fine, Emmalene," then watch his gentle fingers roll a cigarette and light it.

Jakie slept and I sobbed all the way home.

The next day I stood at my back door and looked at the whitening sky, figuring if it would snow. Then I saw Miz Annie driving her horse and buggy around the drive and on the seat next to her was a split white oak basket.

"Thought you might like some stuff we put up." Annie took off her head scarf and heavy cape. "It ain't a whole lot to brag on…just a little something."

She had me a small crock of her family recipe of green cucumber relish, purple jelly from the grapes picked in their backyard arbor, and some of the prettiest golden pear preserves I ever saw.

"I can't thank you enough," I said.

"Your smile is my thanks—like sunbeams jumping from your eyes to your mouth."

"I'm not fit for company," I said, feeling my face get red, "but come on into the front room."

I was glad to point to a big Morris chair that I had fetched down from upstairs, beat out the dust, and left outside in the fresh air for a day. I had laid the doily I crocheted over the back.

We talked for a while about things I was studying: The Blessed Trinity, angels, and Adam and Eve. Some I already knew as my mother had read Bible stories to me when I was little, before she got sick.

"I heard what Eliza did last night," said Annie. "Baptizing Jakie. And you have got a right to be mad at her, but I wanted you to know something that explains her somewhat."

I didn't really care to hear ever what Miz Annie was telling, but I didn't say anything. I had skipped ahead in the catechism to the part, "How to baptize in emergency." I knew exactly what Eliza had been thinking.

"She and Boone got married when Garr and I did. We stood up for each other. But Garr and I have eight children—counting the one that died. And nine counting Les. But poor Eliza. She wanted kids so bad, but lost five in a row. They was born okay, but lay there listless, not moving, not even able to cry. Eliza would sit by the crib and wave a pretty comb, but not one baby opened its eyes to look at its Mama."

When I heard about Eliza's misery, I couldn't hate her anymore. "Miz Annie, I'm sorry as I can be about her trouble, but she still did wrong to baptize my boy — and her and Boone threatening to take him from me."

"No, Boone doesn't let out his sorrow in a mean spirit like Eliza. He just drinks. But he did not ask you to the corn husking to end up trying for Jakie behind your back. I know him too well for that."

Annie told me about Boone's other kindnesses. Besides helping Les get out of Landing Run, he had always been a friend to Garr and all the Richmans. "Why, he lets us use his own plow horses, and puts up our mule that hauls wood for us, and feeds him and Old Sam who is too old to work, and boards them for the winter. And he helps us get in our garden and cornfield..."

She stopped and I reckon she was thinking that their cornfield hadn't even been planted this year, having been sold to Mr. Hershall.

I twisted my hands and looked directly at Miz Annie. "Does ever body think I won't be able to take care of Jakie and the farm and all? Is it like I heard some say, that I need a man to help me?"

"You are a strong and smart woman, Emmalene. If you ask Boone, he can find a sharecropper to go halvies with you, 'cause I don't think you can plow fields and slop hogs and feed cows and take care of Jakie all by yourself."

I hated to think about asking Boone what all I needed to farm my land. It would be more than one time of asking, and I couldn't have people thinking I was trying to take up with yet another woman's man.

It was then I remembered that I'd already asked for Dolin's help to carry things from my shed back to Rice's Store. Although I had forgot all about it after catching Eliza baptizing Jakie.

Miz Annie brightened up and talked about her daughter marrying at Christmas. "Christina told Dolin he ought to tell you first about them getting married before it got spread around."

I sighed.

"Then last night at the corn husking she was too embarrassed to tell anybody."

Annie turned to me, her face kind-hearted as ever I saw. "Emmalene, I know the one who cares for you and nobody knows it but me."

"What do you mean," I said, my mind racing ever which-away.

"All time Les was working for Mr. Hershall, he come home, said he already had his supper and had a peaceful look about him."

Miz Annie's tenderness made me think of my own dear mother, and I wished I had her with me.

"I come to tell you that Boone lit out early this morning and has gone on the train to see Les. After the shucking was over, he told Garr and me and, dang it, I didn't have paper to write Les." Annie put her hand over her mouth and swallowed and then leaned her whole body toward me. "God only knows when Les can come home from Illinois, but it's him that loves you."

I took joy in Annie's words, but couldn't believe it was true. And even if Les did feel that way, and I was free as a newly-made widow, Maribelle still had eyes for him. I remembered hearing what she said to her friends at the shucking party. "Papa is talking to somebody over in Bardstown about getting things straightened out so Les can come back. And Papa wants him to manage his new sawmill."

I had thought Maribelle should keep her mouth shut, but God help me, I strained to hear more.

"And if Papa pays Les good money, then we'll see if I still want to marry him or go board at Nazareth College."

It pained me to think how Maribelle was lying to herself, but I also worried that maybe it was me fooling myself. Yet, here was Les' mother saying she knew his heart and guessing mine.

I ached to talk more about Les. "Of course he wouldn't speak up while I was Mr. Hershall's wife and him working right beside him. But there I was taking care of Dolin and looking out the window to see Les ever day."

Annie dabbed her eyes with the tip of her apron, got up from the table and threw her arms around me. "Dear One, your looks and your ways is giving to people and nobody can help loving you."

After making over Jakie and hugging me again, Annie left for home. I didn't move for the longest time, just sat at the window watching the squirrels running up and down the trees, screeching about all the acorns and nuts they had to store up before winter.

Les
November 1910

Uncle Joe was right pleased with my work—said I was worth two, sometimes three hands because I'm steady and don't go to jabbering and funning around.

I allow the few weeks I'd been in Farmington were jam-packed. After harvesting some awful good corn, I took a load of poultry off, and then we killed four hogs.

It was a cold Saturday night when Boone come driving a wagon and stopped at the horse barn where he saw my lanterns.

"First one I see is who I come to see," said Boone, as he got down from the wagon seat, stretching like he was wore out. I figured he rode the train all day and hired the wagon next morning to drive through to here.

I never knew how much I missed seeing somebody from home til I laid eyes on Boone, who I know as good as I do my own Papa. I put down my currying brush and gave a good pat to the horse, Blackie, I rode most nights. "You're a sight," I said to Boone, and he slapped me on the shoulder.

"I reckon Uncle Joe and them has gone to bed."

"With the chickens. We done a heap this week."

"Come here," Boone said and motioned me to the back of the wagon. He dug into a thick mound of hay and uncovered several gallon jugs and boxes of filled Mason jars all packed in sawdust.

"Old Man Hershall's shine?" I knew the whiskey by sight—I was the one filled the jugs and jars and hid them in a trench I dug myself.

Boone nodded. "I bring a load to Uncle Joe ever year." With a wide grin he popped the cork from a jug and handed it to me for the first drink.

I helped Boone put up his horse, set the whiskey inside the barn, then put away my grooming combs and brushes. I led Blackie to his stall, gave him some water and hay and promised him a better brushing and rubdown next time.

They was a stove in the bunk house, but with the barn doors closed, the wind kept out. The whiskey and the talking kept us warm.

Boone said they'd had the corn shucking at his place the day before and the hog killing would wait til he got back. "Right now, I've paid my workers to help the neighbors gather corn over to Emmalene's and then do the husking as I'm not there to help."

I had to catch myself from blurting out all I wanted to know. I didn't have to ask, for Boone was in a talking mood. He said Cleophus and Jimmy Lee Linkahan had hoed Old Man Hershall's cornfield after he died and never bragged on it. "I don't think Emmalene thought about her own corn what with the old man getting killed. And now, all her other worry."

I wrinkled my eyebrows at Boone.

"I hate to tell it," he said, "but Eliza got it in her head that Jakie being part Cutler—you know, the Old Man's mother—and Eliza herself born a Cutler and a Catholic, she wants to get the boy from Emmalene."

"You ain't allowing that, are you?" I sounded stern to my own self and hoped I wasn't tipping my hand on my feelings. For Emmalene never wrote me back, and it must be Dolin had set out to court her.

Boone took a drink and wiped his mouth. "Nah, my Eliza ain't gonna follow through. After losing all our own babies, she'll figger how it would hurt the girl. Besides, Emmalene is studying to turn Catholic."

My mind jerked in two directions. I didn't know anything about Mr. Hershall's mother, or about Emmalene thinking on getting baptized Catholic, but I wished I could tell Eliza just what I thought about her nasty self. I felt my temper raising and I knew it wouldn't be fitting to yell at Boone over his wife, so I asked a different question: "You heard anything promising about me being clear with the revenuers?"

"You know," he said, "usually the law looks the other way or even down comes on the shine and has a drink with you. But, Son, John L. said he heard an informer gave your name and that's why Sheriff Winters raided the old man's shine."

I wilted like somebody poured hot grease over me. "And he didn't say who turned me in?"

"No. John L. acted like he didn't know. But he said the local constable was being forced by the public prosecutor to gather evidence. Seems like they have to catch somebody sometime to show a good face."

"Do they know where I am?" I asked, thinking maybe I should pack up and move to the south.

"If it was me, I'd stay on with Uncle Joe, for now. He's had a good standing around here for a mighty long time, and he'll keep his mouth shut tight."

I nodded but my heart sunk. Drinking the Old Man's whiskey and hearing about Emmalene needing my help and knowing I had to stay hid like a animal set me to grieving.

"I'd say they'll either indict you or dismiss the case by Christmas or the start of the coming year at the latest."

I looked down at my feet. It wasn't like they didn't treat me good here in Fulton County. Uncle Joe said next spring I could put in my own crop. And Miz Elliott already told me to spend Christmas in their house.

It got me thinking about Christmas and how much it meant to Maw Richman. And the little kids got all excited about a big snow on the ground and Santy Claus coming, and the couples went out courting and caroling in hay-filled wagons and looking at the moonlight on the snow. I was going to miss it all—maybe forever.

During the night, I woke up and found a pencil and some paper. I had to get a letter ready for Boone to carry home to Maw Richman.

> Dear Maw,
> I am fine and hope this finds you all the same. It is almost midnight so please excuse this pothook writing for I am worried over what Boone told me when he got here. He said Eliza is trying to take Jakie away from Emmalene.
> Now, Maw, whatever you do, you go over there and tell her that if she is anything like the Christian she talks about being, she will not go on and do this. For you know how much Emmalene dotes on Jakie.
> Eliza has give our family a lot and you know Boone says he will not allow her doing this awful thing, but you carry a lot of weight with that woman so you stop her.
> Boone said Emmalene is taking instruct to be a Catholic. Now you know if a man who is not Catholic marries her, he would turn one for her.

So I am closing for now. Be sure you talk to Eliza.
Your loving son,
Les

Emmalene
November 1910

I puzzled for two days after Miz Annie left, and decided I would do what had come to me: give her back the cornfield. When Winston McPherson first reminded me that I was its owner after Mr. Hershall died, I felt puffed up over it. But it seemed like, ever time I passed by that bottomland and looked over at the scrub grass and nothing growing, I knew in my heart it still belonged to the Richmans. Mr. Hershall bought it in a mean spirit and I had fought against that bad feeling long enough. Besides, here I was with a farm that I wondered if I could ever manage to grow or sell anything.

Before Boone took off to Illinois to see Les, he promised he'd send some men to gather the corn Mr. Hershall had planted. They wouldn't be coming today, it being Sunday.

I set my mind to go tell Annie that we were making a trip to Bardstown early the next morning. Once I had a good idea, I wanted to act on it right away and we would see my lawyer to get the business done.

Before I got the buggy stopped in front of the Richman house, Nan Mary come a running to take Jakie. Because of his sweet face and long eyelashes I believe all young girls thinks he is their doll. And Jakie just loves when they talk to him and make over him.

Christina told me, "Spect you wanting Mama. She's down at the springhouse."

I walked to the edge of the garden where the path turns downhill, and the trees in back are so thick that no sun comes through to dry up the wet ground.

The rock ledge down the hill was natural wet and dark and I queried myself how in the world Miz Annie could walk down there without any help. I got to the weathered wood door, but I didn't want to open it sudden and scare my friend.

"Annie," I called.

"Wooh," she answered in the way she had of greeting.

As I swung open the door, the wide hinge creaked. The earthy smell of wet underground changed the air I breathed. A natural fountain of water flowed around moss-covered rocks that went from top to bottom of the back of the little wood house. The water spilled down the side rocks and built-in shelves that Garr had fixed, but most of the run-off was carried away by a small waterway. The shelving held crocks of milk, homemade cottage cheese and clabber. On one low plank was some cedar wood boxes with roses Garr had whittled into molds on the undersides of the tops. When Annie took her butter to trade at Rice's Store, her customers would see a pretty rose design on top of it.

"I come to get some sweet cream and some butter," said Annie, holding on to a wood ledge as she leaned in to get them. "Here," she said, and insisted I take one of each for myself.

Annie shook cold water from the fingers of one hand. She had a peaceful look on her face. "Sometimes I get one of the kids to lead me down here and then tell them come back later. And I just stay here and the water music folds me into its song. I let my shoulders slump and all my cares drops away."

I'd seen Annie with her children all calling at once—"Mama, is it anything to eat?" "Mama, can we go out to the swimming hole?" "Mama, she said a bad word, uh huh." Even Garr would sometimes quiz her, "Annie, where'd you say you put my clean shirt?"

Everything so quiet in my house with Jakie saying nary a word, and then no quiet for Annie with all the goings on. It seemed like one trip down here a day might not be enough.

With our hands full we turned to leave, avoiding water spilling from the spring that kept the rock floor wet.

"Oh, Emmalene, you gotta have a good, cold drink of water before we go. It's the best taste in the world."

I couldn't hardly wait to tell her what I was going to do, but I got down the tin cup hanging from a nail on the edge of a shelf and dipped it into a clear pool of water. I held the cup and drank and she was right. There was no better water anywhere, and she had a right to brag.

I closed the springhouse door behind us and Annie started up the hill in front of me.

She told me about coming to this same springhouse ever since she could remember. "My great-grandparents had this natural spring dug out and lined it with rocks in the deepest part of a running pool. They built the little wooden shed around it, same time they put up the log house up that hill where they raised their kids."

The Richman house looked like many in Landing Run—two big log rooms with a built-in hall between them, and a long front porch. Of an evening, the family gathered after supper to sit in the cooler air away from the kitchen and listen to the farm animals quieting down in the barn, the frogs croaking by the creek, and the whippoorwills crying in the woods.

"Mama signed it all over to me, but I think of this place as still hers and it will be hers…I hope til a long time from now," said Annie.

She pointed up toward their home, the barn and outbuildings. "My Grandmaw and Grandpaw was married in 1817 by Reverend John David, who became Bishop David two years later. You probably know he came from France with Bishop Flaget to minister to the first Catholics here."

Father Donnelly had told me about the Catholics from St. Mary's County in Maryland who had settled mainly in three central Kentucky counties.

We stepped careful-like and Annie pointed to a spongy pad of moss beside the rock ledge. She bent down to look close at a dark green circle of toadstools.

"It's a fairy ring," she said, laughing. "I made wishes on them when I was young, but I don't reckon they come out dancing once you're grown-up."

It struck me odd that Annie would ever believe in fairies or making wishes or seeing signs. What I learned so far was the church said not to put trust in such. But then again, they was all in favor of saying a nine-day prayer, the Novena, or asking St. Anthony to find anything lost or praying to St. Jude for hopeless cases. And like the time she said she prayed to St. Anne that she wouldn't get pregnant again, then the next month found out she was gonna have Nace.

I never had a doubt that Annie was a good woman, and whenever things didn't go right, she'd straighten up her shoulders and say, "It's God's will."

We were almost to the top where it was level ground, when Annie's shoe slipped and I grabbed her while still holding onto the box of butter and jar of cream.

Annie breathed hard and her shoulders trembled while she looked at me, her face screwed up and close to mine.

I blurted out, "I'm signing the cornfield back over to you!"

For a little while Annie seemed like she was not going to get another good breath. "Oh, Emmalene, you can't do that," she finally said.

It took a while to make her understand that nothing else would make me happy and she finally agreed only when I said okay, that

they would pay it back if they ever could.
	We made it up that we would go to file with the Recording Clerk in Bardstown the next day.

Les
November 1910

Next morning, Boone ate a big breakfast with his aunt and uncle and they made me eat with them. Boone wouldn't stay a second night, just pocketed the money Uncle Joe give him for the whiskey.

"Emmalene sure can use this," he said to me as he hooked up the horse to the empty wagon.

I gave him my letter to Maw, shook his hand, wished him well and said tell ever body hey.

"After I turn in this rig, I got another long train ride ahead of me." Boone reached into his coat pocket. "I almost forgot. Dolin was one of the last to leave after the husking and he give me this letter for you."

Boone turned the wagon east and rode away. I saw that Dolin had scribbled something on the back of a bank receipt of Boone's.

Emmalene
November 1910

"I have never been to Bardstown without Garr Richman since we married!" Annie said. But she seemed happy to be setting out with me, just us women, on a adventure to see a big-shot lawyer.

She had on her black wool cape that fastened at the neck, and had a loose-fitting hood. Her street boots was greased black and buttoned all up to the ankle.

I wore my self-same rose-colored dress, but it was hid with the fitted burgundy frock coat I wore in from the mountains. It was warm wool with a long row of buttons down the front and slits in the back We both wore our church hats, kind of wide around, but no flowers or feathers.

Before we left, the Richman kids wrapped hot rocks in old blankets to set our feet on, and we both had buggy robes against the cold air. Our feet still got cold before long, as well as our ears and noses, but we talked a mile a minute, and soon there we was at Courthouse Square.

I was struck again by how pretty the building was with the late morning sun shining on its red bricks and white trellis paneling and a breeze blowing the flag hanging from the tall pole in front. Annie said it was just rebuilt in 1892.

Catty-corner was the law office building. It had rows of long windows with many glass panes on the first and second floor. There was chimneys at both ends and a big sign over the front door in the center reading: JUDD, SMITH & MCPHERSON.

Annie and me sat and looked at the place, both lost in our thoughts. After a minute I stood up. "Winston McPherson is my lawyer and he gets paid for his service, so we needn't feel low-station to go in that fancy building."

Annie got up strong, and with me guiding her, we fairly pranced to the front door.

A tall, skinny man answered my knock and led us down a long hallway to Mr. McPherson's office.

I had not forgotten how fine he looked when he rode his horse to my farm and read Mr. Hershall's will to me. He came around from his desk, smiling bigger than ever, wearing a dark, high-buttoned suit with a white shirt collar starched and standing up against his chin. He sure looked different from men we saw at church dressed in their best overalls with the cuffs turned up, long-sleeve shirts buttoned at the collar, and big tie-up work shoes.

Mr. McPherson came up close to me, gave a short bow and he smelled like soap and talcum powder. I introduced him to Annie, and he tilted his head a bit saying, "So very nice to meet you, Ma'am."

The skinny man waited at the door.

"Bring us some tea, John. With cream, sugar and lemon."

Then Mr. McPherson asked Annie about the weather and our trip to town while I gazed around the room. The fireplace had small red coals burning and the mantel piece had wood inlay and hand-painted flowers on the tiles.

Near the door stood a wooden hat and coat rack with a mirror at the top, but Annie and I said no thanks to hanging up our wraps.

When John brought in the tea, I ended up unfastening my coat and Annie her cloak and we laid them across the tops of our chairs.

On a small table between us, John set down the waiter tray which held white china cups, saucers, spoons, and a polished pewter set of tea pot, sugar bowl and creamer, all with curving handles.

Annie said, "I thank you kindly, but I don't drink tea."

I felt bad for thinking maybe she was too scared to handle the tiny cup, or feared she'd set hers down too hard on the little plate. Maybe she was afraid she would slop cream on the table or turn something over.

My hands looked red when I took my cup from John, but I didn't let that stop me from putting in sugar and cream and tasting how good it was.

"Mr. McPherson," I said.

"Please. You must call me Winn."

It was hard to get out his name with Annie sitting there and maybe thinking I was being too free and easy with him.

Getting the title of the cornfield transferred from me to Miz Annie was simple. John, the secretary for the group of lawyers in the building, typed up the document, so Winn just had to fill in the blanks.

He took a gold-nibbed fountain pen from a crystal inkwell and held it easy like it was no more than a pencil nub. I couldn't help but get my eyes full of the things on his desk, ever bit as fine as his pen and ink—a tobacco pouch of soft leather, a briar pipe and a silver lighter.

"Emmalene, I have the exact location of the property and your legal name and address from your file. Mrs. Richman, all I need to know is if you are married or not, and your address to mail the deed."

Annie and I looked at each other, both of us smiling.

"There is the consideration of sale," said Winn. "If this is a gift, we shall use one dollar as a formality."

I drew in my breath, not wanting Annie to be embarrassed for lack of a dollar. But, bless her heart, she pulled a dollar bill from her pocket and with her head up and shoulders back, handed it to Winn.

In the blank for amount of sale, he wrote, "One dollar, Love and Affection." He turned to Miz Annie. "As you are the grantee, I will send the deed to you once I have taken it to the Recorder's Office. And I will do that henceforth." And he handed me the dollar.

Winn walked us to the door of his office and John took us down the shiny wood floors of the hallway to the front door and opened it. Then he stood back.

"Have a good day, Ladies," he said, and he smiled sort of friendly like.

"Oh, we will," laughed Annie.

As we walked along the driveway, I tried to give back her dollar, but she turned and faced me. "No, indeedy, you will not give that back! You absolutely will not!"

With the sun shining on her gray hair and her sparkling face, she hugged me hard.

My buggy horse danced about, springing from her hind legs all way out of Bardstown. Her spirits seemed as high as Annie's and mine.

"You don't know how much we appreciate getting back that sweet little meadow," Annie said, patting my arm.

She couldn't know how light and easy I felt after signing it over. We talked and laughed like never before, and directly we got to the turn-off in front of Boone's.

"This is Monday afternoon," said Annie, "and Eliza is sure to be out there in her back yard a finishing up her wash. Turn in here! Let's get this thing about Jakie settled once and for all!"

I dreaded having to face Eliza Boone, but I knew the whole thing had to come to a boil sooner or later, so I pulled my right rein a little tighter, and my horse made the turn, still happy.

As we drove through the lane of trees and up to where the fences began, we smelled the pig pens. Yes, it was Eliza's washday, for driving back to the farmhouse we saw sheets blowing out from the clotheslines like sails on a ship and her battling the dirt out of a pair of Boone's overalls. Close by was a big iron pot of water simmering on a fire grate, with wood chips a burning under it. On a workbench set one big tub filled with steaming, soapy water and another, probably with cold rinse water. A cut-off barrel of water was at the end—for a second rinse.

Eliza looked up from her work and wiped her hands on her apron.

I lighted from the buggy first and saw Eliza's eyes was the only thing moving. She had to wonder at us all dressed up on a Monday.

"We just come from the lawyer's office," said Annie, her voice chirpy and her eyes gleaming.

Eliza slumped down on the end of her workbench and put her hands on her chest. Her mouth hung open.

"You'll never guess my good luck," Annie said. "Emmalene, dear girl that she is, has deeded back the lost cornfield to me."

I could see relief spelled out on Eliza's face and it come to me that she was jarred thinking I was getting up a case about keeping Jakie. For a minute, I thought I had passed up my chance and should have done just that.

But Annie was quick to jump in, her face stern now. "Eliza, we dropped by to see if you was really trying to get Jakie away from Emmalene. We need to have this settled right here."

I already had my answer, for Eliza was shaking her head back and forth, back and forth. "No—no I am not. I am sorry such a thing got spread around for it has grieved me and Boone to think it all got out of hand." She twisted her hands in her apron. "Yes, I did check on the birth records at the church and traced that Mr. Hershall's mother was a Cutler and some kin to me from a couple generations back. But I never took it any further, having come to my senses."

I stood stock still waiting for her to bring up that I was no kin to Jakie, but she just sat there and hanged her head.

Annie went over and hugged her. "There now, well, that's good to know. We can finally put a stop to the talk."

With her eyelids fluttering like she had to force them to meet my eyes, Eliza said, "Emmalene, I want to tell you…well, it ain't no good enough excuse but it's just when a person grieves long enough they go crazy. And I sure acted crazy and I hope you won't hold it agin me forever."

I nodded at her, not really knowing if she was being truthful. I smiled to be nice, but I questioned if she really was gonna change how she treated me, and how long it would take me to believe her.

The air seemed a little strained for a minute, then Annie whooped, "Look at that sun already passed way over the house! I gotta get home and start supper and, Eliza, you got wash to finish up."

Before long, Annie and I was in the buggy and riding back out to Landing Run Road, our excitement still high.

When we got to the Richman house, Annie insisted I come in and eat with them. After our good day together, I didn't want to leave her either.

Emmalene
December 1910

Pretty soon, my women friends was treating me like we'd known each other from the beginning. It wasn't no surprise when Annie rode over on her horse—Old Sam—and told me to get ready, for Eliza was having a quilting bee.

They was a four-piece quilting frame set up on the backs of chairs in Eliza's parlor with the Double Wedding Ring quilt latched in place. Its top was little pieces of goods cut and sewed together making shapes of rings locking inside one another—same in pattern but different in color. Eliza had been working on it by herself and the top was already basted to the lining and its inside batting. There was big basting stitches all around the edges and crossways from the middle to hold the three layers together for the real quilting.

Each of us women had been sewing little patchwork blocks of the six-sided Honeycomb pattern at home and would piece them together for the next quilt top. With eight or ten women working all day and getting our dinner cooked by the hired girls in Eliza's kitchen, we counted on finishing up both quilts.

Annie and Christina was the center of attention, for these beautiful bed covers was being made for Christina's hope chest. Annie was just as proud as if the quilts were for herself and smiled as she bent her face close to the frame.

"These will make the bed look so pretty," Christina said, her eyes bright and face turning pink when she ran her fingers over the fabric of many colors. "Either one would make a Sunday Quilt for company."

What a buzz us women was making when we first sat down, either around the quilting frame or on the floor sorting blocks of pieced material. It was like looking at a scrapbook with one recognizing the goods from a threadbare dress whose sleeve was still strong, while another spotted what was left from new apron material. We had as much fun trading scraps and patterns as we did giving the quilts to one or the other.

After a hour or so, Eliza served us cake on her white china dishes with light pink roses painted on their edges. They wasn't any more beautiful than her three layer cake with high-fluffed white icing. She poured cold milk for us, and even on a chilly day it went real good with the sweet cake.

Eliza said, "Emmalene, you're a good quilter making those stitches small and even. Why don't you start out here beside me? We can wrap the closest edges on the roller and turn the quilt under as we go."

I remembered Mother letting me help her with the quilting when I was little bitty. I wished she was looking down from Heaven and feeling proud that here I was a grown woman at a sewing bee with the ladies in Landing Run.

By late afternoon we had been telling stories and laughing til it didn't seem like we was working. I enjoyed myself so much I didn't think of milking time til Boone came to the parlor door. He looked straight at me and gave a nod like he wanted to talk to me.

I didn't even put down my thimble, just gathered up my skirts and went to him. He had a serious look. "I just did your milking, Emmalene, and as I started home I saw two men on horseback turn into your lane."

I never thought to say thank you, just asked quick, "Who was it?"

"Well, I don't know. They looked like they'd rode for quite a piece, both them and the horses wore down. One had light hair, real kinky, and the other had straight black hair growing long as his beard.

"Jarboe!" I said the name out loud, for tight, curly, whitish looking hair had to be him. And the other was one of my step-brothers, for it sounded like Hack or Conrad either one.

Annie walked into the kitchen where we stood. "Anything wrong?"

"I gotta go home. Would you tell Eliza I had a real good time?"

It didn't take me long to get Jakie from where he played with Nan Mary who was keeping watch over several little ones. My heart was not joyful, but scared. I wasn't fond of seeing either of the Fielding boys or Jarboe after all this time.

I had never told Jarboe that I was marrying Mr. Hershall to get away from him. My step-father, Everett Fielding, being kin to the old man by marriage, had agreed to let me go away and even rode with us down the side of the mountain to where the preacher waited at the general store.

That day, I became a Hershall and left everything I knew, which is what I wanted. I decided I could escape the memories of lying on a grassy hillside, planning a life in the mountains with the boy I thought I knew so well.

First thing I saw at my house was that cotton top of Jarboe's coming out of the rain barrel at my kitchen door. He splashed and spluttered, making so much noise he didn't see me.

I sat in the buggy stone still and couldn't believe he was here in Nelson County. All the pain he had dealt me came flooding in and my heart hurt. At the same time, just looking at his wet muscled arms and chest a glistening in the sun took me back to a hundred sweet times.

He had brought happiness to me when I felt like I didn't belong where I lived. I was ten years old when my paw died in a coal mine accident and Mother was pretty near bound by need to marry Ernest Fielding, who also had to have help raising his sons. Hack and Conrad thought mostly about their hunting dogs and acted like I wasn't even there. So I never did care for them as good as brothers.

The part I did like about Mother marrying again was the Fieldings lived in the same holler as Jarboe.

In the old days of fall weather, we walked up the mountainside into the deep shady woods where the ginseng grows. Jarboe searched out the sang roots big around as his finger and strips of slippery elm bark for his maw's bitters, while I gathered my arms full of wild daisies. He made me feel important when he asked what I thought about why the sky was blue and if dreams came to us from spirits or was they of our own making. His nature was sunny and he made me feel like somebody worthy whenever I was with him.

My horse whinnied and brought me back to myself. Two horses in the barn nickered back. That's when Jarboe saw my buggy.

"Hidy, Emmalene," he said wiping off his face and arms. He grinned big and walked over to me.

"What are you doing here?" I asked him, hoping my tone was more frosty than I felt.

Jarboe wiped under his arms and squinted his eyes up at me, still laughing. "Somehow that don't sound like you're proud to see me."

"After you turned around and married some other body, I never thought to lay eyes on you again."

"Can't you even light down from the buggy and come inside and see your brother who's come over holler and ridge to visit?"

Stepbrother, I said to myself.

About that time Hack come out the kitchen door with a jar of jam in one hand and a hunk of leftover cornbread in the other.

Something agitated inside me, when he dug a big spoon into Miz Annie's blackberry jam that she give me.

He smacked his lips tasting ever bit of the sweetness. "Well, I be jiggered. My little sister is all growed up."

It wasn't in me to tell them to go on away from here, much as I felt like it. It was something about them making theirselves to home that didn't set right. After I fried up some ham meat and baked another pan of biscuit, they sprawled out in the front room.

Hack eased on down in the best chair and propped up his feet on Jakie's stool. Little Jakie hung onto my skirts, not like he was scared but maybe wary of two strangers here at once. I was cautious my own self.

Getting warm and drowsy in front of the fire, they told whatever news came to mind—that being what they reckoned as fun: boys turning over privies at Halloween, taking younger fellers snipe hunting and leaving them by their selves to wait in the dark. And going to the Pentecost church, and just when a feller got the ghost, they let loose a billy goat to run inside.

Both of them laughed so hearty I figured they couldn't help theirselves, wore down from days of riding, and some at night, all the way from Clay County.

Jarboe wandered around the room looking close at the clock on the mantel and the cloth edge I'd embroidered. He picked up my Baltimore Catechism and made out the words "Roman Catholic Church."

"What you doing with this here?" he said, holding the book out toward me.

I glared him in the face and his looks was even better than last I saw him. His light beard was stubbly and I remembered how he used to nuzzle against my cheek just to hear me complain and tell him, "Stop it!" Yet I didn't feel like I did then—what he done made him unfit as my beau.

"Catlicks eats kids, you know."

I sneered at him, wanting him to see my scorn.

Hack lifted a pint jar ever few minutes, and before long his breath came hard and he started in to snoring loud and long.

I put Jakie to bed with two warm covers over him. All time I fidgeted, uneasy about where I would tell the men to sleep and wondering how long they aimed to stay. I couldn't make out which one had the idea to come here.

When I got back to the fire, Jarboe brought his chair next to mine and whispered, "I got a thing to tell you." I feared his serious turn.

My mind jumbled, for I wanted mighty bad to ask about his married life, how was his wife and if the baby was born, but I hadn't wanted ever thing said out in front of Hack and let him in on my innermost feelings.

"I never married," Jarboe said in a low tone, although there was no need—Hack was dead asleep.

"Truth of the business is, that girl ran out on me. Up and took off with somebody else who she told me was the actual daddy of her baby."

I sat still as a statue. Jarboe never married. I could have stayed in the mountains and become his wife and never knew the troubles here in Nelson. But another thought took over—how pleasurable I felt to escape a untrue love and find my new self in Landing Run. Warm feelings rushed through my body, and it was that moment I knew the change in my heart was real. I had become a part of the Catholics all around me in this blessed countryside.

Jarboe reached out a hand to touch me and I jumped up fast. "I'll get you the counterpane off my bed and you can sleep here by the fireplace," I said.

"Well now, hold on, Emmalene. You ain't heard what I come to ask of you."

That simmering fear I had held ever since I saw him had struck a boil.

"What?" I said and didn't even care if my voice was harsh.

"I got my pride hurt by the woman I thought I would marry, and that made me feel right sorry about how I was false to you." He put up his hand to stop me from speaking. "I ain't got no shame, for I'm here to tell you I have lived hard without a true love and I want to carry you back to Clay County to be my wife."

I stood there and wanted mighty bad to say something smart-alec, something to hurt him like he hurt me. But as I looked at him, I found I didn't need to add misery to his sad and wishful face.

Times without number I had pined to hear these words from the man in front of me. But I had scoured all thought of Jarboe from my heart, as it about made me sick to think of how I had loved him and had to put many miles and many months between us. Yet here time was reaching back and bringing itself around to right now, though I didn't expect it nor want it.

"Those days have passed," I said. "I am a widow woman with Jakie and a good farm to take care of, and I don't aim to ever go back to the mountains, for this is my home. I thank you for the asking, but I'm not marrying you."

Jarboe stared at the floor a bit, then grunted a laugh like he took my full meaning. "Then you ain't gonna like what Hack has to say." He nodded toward the sleeping man.

"Hack wants the farm. Says he is second cousin to Jakie through his pap being brother to Old Man Hershall's first wife."

My body shook. I wanted to take up the poker and light into both of them for coming here trying to pull this over on me.

"Now hold on," Jarboe said, standing up. "He says if you didn't want to leave here with me, then he would marry you since you all ain't no blood kin. That way the farm would be kept in the family."

I clenched my teeth but was still fairly screaming. "I ain't marrying neither the one of you and I ain't signing over my farm! You see to it that you all strike out of here before the sun comes up tomorrow morning!" I took a step toward Hack. "And rouse him and the both of you sleep in the barn loft!"

Jarboe took a long breath, then nodded toward Hack. "I don't reckon as how I can sleep with that braying all night."

I took no mind. "They's plenty saddle blankets in the barn."

Real fast I got the bed cover and threw it to Jarboe, and near run to my room.

They was a keyhole in my bedroom door but weren't no key to it I ever saw. Plenty times I had thought about buying a long brass key at Rice's to see if it would fit that door but never carried it through. Now, it appeared like I should've.

I didn't have a straight chair in my room to jamb up under the door knob, so I pushed the footrail of my bed as close as I could get it to the door. If either of those jaybirds tried to get in, at least it would stop them for a while. I wished it was morning and they was already gone.

I didn't sleep for straining to hear any undue noises in the night. I knew by heart the outside who-who-who of the barred owl, the crying of a whippoorwill in the woods, the thrump, thrump, thrump of tree frogs—it was the footfalls of a man's boots that I was fearful of. For after what Jarboe told me, either one of them was thinking to marry me to get the farm legal. And as I refused both, it was no telling what they would try next.

I didn't have an idee what time it was when there come a knock on my door. I must have been asleep, for the first thought I had was, it being Sunday, I had to get up and get Jakie and me ready for Mass. This morning the first banns was gonna be read for Christina and Dolin.

I got up quiet as I could and squeezed myself between the bed and the door, bracing my butt against the bottom foot rail and holding the door closed with my hand on the knob.

It was Hack at the door.

"Listen, here, Girl. You said no to going back to Clay County and marrying Jarboe and letting me handle the farm."

By the light of soft glowing coals in the fireplace in my room, I looked at Jakie in his built-in bed. He was still sleeping, dear boy.

"This farm needs a man and I need a farm, and me being the old man's nephew, it's more rightful mine than yours."

I didn't answer, hoping he would think I was still asleep, but he turned the knob from outside and I held tight. He must have thought it was locked.

"I know you hear me. Now let me in so I don't have to force this door!"

I thought about Mr. Hershall's shotgun I had stored in the locked room upstairs where I couldn't get to it and didn't know how to shoot, anyway. I pictured the small amount of cash money I had in a pillowcase and stuffed between the feather ticks on my bed, but figgered it wasn't enough payment for him to leave.

I yelled against the door, "You get gone from here, Hack Fielding! I am Mr. Hershall's legal widow and he left me the farm and the care of Jakie, and it's all written down at my lawyer's!"

"Whoop-de-do! What's the law and what's right is two different things! Did Jarboe tell you that if you didn't want to leave here, you and me can get married since they's no blood between us?"

"You are pure crazy! Now the two of you saddle up and get back to your home and I'm staying here in mine!"

"I ain't aiming to hurt you. I got my pants on—I just think you ought to know you'd get a man who'd dig in to work for you, and make a husband and a pappy for Jakie, if you'd only listen." He pushed harder against the door and I was so mad, all my strength battled against him to hold the door shut. He quit turning the knob, but I could hear him breathing.

"You got my answer, Hack. Now ride out of here!"

I was so close to my door I could hear the sounds of him drinking and swallowing and screwing the cap back on a jar.

He walked away for a while and I breathed a little better but couldn't totally go limp for fear he would come back and throw his whole body against the door which he would not only get in but maybe break my arms or legs.

He did come back again, but this time a wheedling. "C'mon now, Emmalene. You know your maw and Uncle Notice, God rest his soul, would want you and me together to look out for one another. You don't have to lay down with me."

It made me mad for Hack to mention my mother, but I just stood there gripping the doorknob and fuming inside.

It came pure daylight and everything had got still but I kept holding the door. Hack came up again and said, "They's ice on the grass this morning," just like we hadn't been battling like what seemed half the night.

I never answered, just stood ready to push against the door if he turned the knob. In the stillness, I heard horses and buggy wheels in my driveway. Then the wooden floorboards in the kitchen creaked and the door was swung open and I knew it must be Hack had gone to see who was there.

I heard Boone's voice loud and clear. "Where's Emmalene?"

Not even grabbing my shawl, I pushed past Hack and stepped into the chill air. "I'm okay," I said. "This is my step-brother, which him and his friend are just heading back to Clay County."

Boone sat on his horse, and nodded his head slow. Standing there in a row beside him was Dr. Beale in his buggy, John L. Meadors and Albert Nobles both on horses.

"You weren't at church this morning so we thought we'd check up on you," said Dr. Beale.

I turned my head to see Jarboe leading his saddled horse toward the kitchen.

Boone gave a strong look at Hack. "We'll ride out to Jackson Highway with you all—to make sure you find your way back home."

Hack stood for half a minute looking from Boone who had a rifle strapped in a gun rug on his saddle, to Dr. Beale who smoked his cigar easy-like, to Albert who had a mean look on his face. Hack stepped in the house, got his hat and coat, and walked to the barn to saddle his horse.

Jarboe talked to the men, and I thought to get my shawl before I shook to death. While I passed the kitchen, I put some leftover ham meat and biscuit bread in a meal sack for them. No need to send them off hungry, even if I was mad and wasn't likely to get over it anyways soon.

It started snowing the morning of Christmas Eve. Seemed like Jakie and me was always over to Miz Annie's, and there we sat helping get Christina's wedding clothes finished and something for the Richman kiddies and Jakie from Old Santy.

Father Donnelly had announced the banns of matrimony between Dolin and Christina for three Sundays in a row, and with my corn got in by the neighbors, I felt like I would have a pretty nice Christmas. Especially since I got a good-size credit at Rice's Store after Dolin carried back all Mr. Hershall's stuff from the shed.

Annie had dressed two big old hens for roasting, and there would be three parties—one for the kids before Mass when Santy Claus left presents, and one for the young people going out caroling, and another after midnight when we'd all celebrate Christina and Dolin being new marrieds.

The only thing wrong was, Les couldn't come home. That put a damper on our good times. We'd been blue ever since Boone got back from seeing Les. He gave me all the money he got after selling the rest of the moonshine the revenuers didn't find, but the case against Les was still up in the air.

One nice thing, though. Eliza had been speaking so nice to me. She wasn't the same person, touching my arm and smiling, and it near broke my heart to see her bend down to talk to Jakie and see the longing in her eyes. She ran her hands over his hair and softly patted his coat collar and told Boone, "Give this good little boy a nickel."

I had to watch that Jakie didn't put it in his mouth, for he never pondered what a nickel was for.

Annie had told me that Boone brought her a short letter from Les after getting home from his visit to Illinois, but she didn't offer to let me read it. She had just said she wished it was safe to answer Les, but Boone said it was best not to. He said the case was coming up in a short while and we'd be better off praying Les gets released than to write just yet.

Going into the Richman house lifted my spirits with it smelling all fresh of cedar branches and sweet, spicy holiday clove balls, which was whole apples and lemons studded with cloves. Over the fireplace was hung bunches of holly with red berries and spiny-pointed leaves. The fireplace was the center of the Richman home for it was used to cook and to keep warm. Sitting on the hearth was a stone crock of hot apple cider sweetened with maple syrup.

The kids hung pine wreaths tied with red cloth bows on the front door and spread the inside window ledges with bunches of pinecones held together with ribbons.

Miz Annie said I was a comfort to her—I think because I told her my heart belonged to Les. She treated me like a daughter, and I ate it up like berries and sugar.

"What more can we give Christina and Dolin?" she asked.

"I think them bedclothes you did up are right nice." I ran my hands over the smooth white sheeting and pillowcases edged with blue scallops. They sure looked fancy laying on top of Christina's hope chest.

Annie sighed. "I just wish we could come up with more, but I only been able to put a few cents in the red jar in the kitchen. And that's for time of need."

Grandmaw Greenhaven sat with me and Annie in front of the fireplace, all of us sewing. Annie sat nearest the lamp, even in daylight, and brought her sewing up close to her face.

Truth of it, Grandmaw outdid us both as she knitted ever day. She sat in her rocker, her eighty-one-year-old face a picture of happiness, having her daughter and all the grandchildren around her, all loving her like they did. "All I've got to do is finish up the mittens and socks. When we wrap everything in pretty cloth and spread it under the tree, the kids will throw a fit over surprises from Old Santy Claus."

I glanced through the doorway at the kitchen table. Christina and Nan Mary had spread an oilcloth to protect a hicker-nut cake and Annie's special jam cake with caramel icing. Christina looked in the oven at her big biscuits, ready to fill with slices of boiled ham.

Caroling would start come nightfall and the fixings were for the young people who would go door to door, waking up neighbors with fiddle music and singing and dancing. Garr had his gallon jugs of elderberry wine up from the cellar, ready to carry with them.

Annie warned her husband, but her voice sounded all happy and loving, "Don't you get out there and drink too much, for this night you are going to church with us, and I don't want your breath stinking and you acting a fool."

I rubbed the silvery gray of Christina's wedding suit against my cheek. Annie had got it in a trade at Rice's after months of saving up a pillowcase full of washed goose feathers to swap. It was the best wool Miz Rice had—so soft it felt like cotton.

Grandmaw called Christina in for the last fitting, and the tall girl shifted from foot to foot. Christina looked awkward up side little Nan Mary, and although she was the oldest and the biggest, she was afraid of the dark. I was surprised to hear that she hung onto Nan Mary's skirt while going upstairs to the loft where they slept.

"Don't you all take so much pains for me, Mama," Christina said, but I noticed that it had tickled her to watch ever step of the dressmaking, from the pieces being cut out from a homemade pattern to the fittings.

Annie told me Christina admired her new clothes ever day. "When nobody's looking, she goes to the bureau and runs her hands over each sleeve of her ivory blouse and its lace eyelet insert." Her wedding outfit made the prettiest clothes she'd ever owned.

"This suit is going to last you a lifetime," Annie said to her daughter. "There's a give in the goods and when you go to having a little one, it'll make it more roomy. You can go to church without anybody noticing."

Christina's face turned red and she hurried to put on her coat to leave when Garr came in with an axe over his shoulder.

"Who wants to go get the Christmas tree?" Garr's face screwed up in pain as he lifted his arms to straighten the toboggan on his head.

Outside in the lane beside the Richman house, the horse stamped up and down and switched his tail high like he knew something fun was gonna happen.

The wagon left for the woods, the children fairly screaming with joy and ringing cowbells while the wheels crunched new ruts in the snow.

Us women took up sewing again for the kids, who would, like every Christmas Eve, be looking to find Santy's gifts.

Annie sewed the last button on Christina's wedding coat. "One thing," she said, "I believe our girl is getting a good man who loves her. Blind as I am, I see how Dolin's eyes cherish her."

I was glad for the couple, too, seeing how they were together. He would pat her arm and push a stray piece of hair back into the bun on her neck, and Christina would knock his hand away, saying, "Don't." But I noticed she bloomed whenever he paid her attention.

When they brought the tree from the woods, Dolin was with them. He is the one who chopped off bottom branches to fit into a stand and set up the tree. Christina slid a iron skillet of popcorn back and forth over a grate in the fireplace, and the kids strung it into white ropes to put on the tree. We crisscrossed them with strings of red buck berries. Also, they was stars made of bright material, jar lids pasted with pictures cut from a catalog, and little candles with tiny clips to hang on the branches.

Annie told Dolin, "You're going to be part of the family at midnight, so you get to place the angel on the tip-top." It was the special angel Grandmaw had made from a leftover piece of blue goods. It had wings made from haywire and hair of yellow yarn.

Soon Dolin went home to help decorate the Linkahan tree for his last time as a single man with Bertie, his brothers, and Uncle James.

Garr had gone over to Boone's to see if he was back from Bardstown with news of Les. Boone thought maybe Judge McPherson would have the case before him today.

The kids played with Jakie in the snow. Miz Annie, Grandmaw and me was hurrying to finish making cornhusk dolls for the little girls while listening to the fireplace hiss and spark when the wind whistled, drafting up the chimney.

We had got quiet and it was then we heard bells tinkling in the lane beside the house. And some kind of music. It sounded like an accordion squeezebox, but we didn't know the foreigner tune. Kind of sad and homesick, yet joyful in its way.

I couldn't help smiling. Christmas Eve Day and a traveling peddler!

Annie and me put on our scarves and coats and walked outside, where we saw a wagon painted bright blue and red, pulled by one horse. Copper bells on the horse halter caught the sun.

When the wagon got close, I saw the peddler wore a long black coat over a white shirt and dark trousers. His beard and coat about covered his vest. He wore a felt hat low on his forehead, just above his eyes, and black hair curled from around his ears into his beard.

Christina carried Jakie, and Nan Mary and all the kids quit playing in the snow and came toward the wagon.

The peddler unstrapped his accordion and climbed down.

I had heard that Jewish people were gypsies that stole children and chickens, but I didn't believe it. They also said that in Louisville the shopkeepers would stand out on the street and grab men by their arms and pull them into their stores.

Mother had always told me that although dark-faced foreigners couldn't speak good English, they hunkered down and worked hard helping each other out. So it didn't matter if they prayed from prayer books different from the Bible. They was good people.

Mr. Hershall had never talked bad about the Jewish men who travel this countryside selling goods from rolling stores. He once told me they worked ever bit as long hours as the farmers and had it extry hard being away from home for weeks at a time.

The man who stepped from the wagon didn't take off his hat, just touched the brim. He showed respect, speaking to Annie. "Good day, Madam. Is husband home?" He stepped careful into the snow-filled lane, stamping his rubber galoshes. The metal snaps jingled.

His short sentences and clear way of saying things sounded different from the kind of talk I had always heard, either in the mountains or here in Landing Run.

Annie walked closer and told him her husband would be back directly. The peddler stood shorter than her and tilted his face up to talk. He was dark-complected and had real white teeth. I watched his eyes lighten up when the children moved a little closer to his wagon.

"Come, come. Yes. Look," the man said to the Richman kids and Jakie.

Foster ducked his head but couldn't hide a grin.

Annie smiled at the peddler. She sounded embarrassed about the little ones' wet clothes and messy hair sticking out from their caps after tumbling around in the snow. "I wished I'd a known you was coming here, for I could have gotten the kids to wash up and put on Sunday shoes."

"See fine things, same as in city store," the man said, nodding his head toward me and Annie. I stood close enough to recognize onions and garlic on his breath and the sweat rising from his wool suit. His manly smells, also of pipe tobacco and wood smoke, did not displease me.

Foster brushed snow off the side of the wagon and finger-traced the bright curlicues on red and blue painted pictures. "You talk different, but I like it," he said.

The Jewish man smiled. "I bring family to America from small village in Ukraine."

"Is that across the ocean?"

"Yes. Very far." The peddler chuckled, looking at the little ones who hovered around him and his painted wagon, eyes and mouths open.

"Everything for home," he said to Annie, spreading his hand toward the wagon.

Annie said she didn't have money to buy anything, but the dark man shook his head. "You look, little ones look."

Christina touched the accordion laying on the seat and Foster petted the horse. Nan Mary went to the back and climbed inside. She picked up a set of blue-speckled granite pans, a wooden biscuit board, a flour sifter and a rolling pin. She and Christina began to exchange items, too excited to look close at any one thing.

Nan Mary pulled quilt wrappings from a box of oranges near the back of the wagon. They had a golden glow. Oh, how I wished I could get one for Jakie and for each Richman for Christmas. I didn't remember how long it was since I tasted a sweet juicy orange.

"You all be careful now and don't handle those things," Annie warned.

I could tell she felt bad for the peddler's waste of time here, yet she couldn't bring herself to tear the children away.

The dark man stepped well back from the wagon, into the stacked snow off the driveway. He stood smiling, wiping his face with a big handkerchief.

His delight in the joy of the children touched me. I wanted to buy something, anything to reward him for his kindness. I didn't have money with me, and I had to be saving with what I had hid in my mattress.

Standing at the back of the wagon, Christina looked at the kitchen things hanging from wires in the ceiling. The girl was getting married that night but didn't have her own home to set up housekeeping. I knew there must be other things that she'd want to lay in her hope chest beside the quilts, hand-sewn bedding, tea towels and hooked potholders given her by relatives and neighbors.

Looking in open boxes, Christina admired an oil lamp in a brass holder, with its glass lampshade etched in white, "Home Sweet Home." She lifted two heavy black flatirons. For now, she didn't need them as she and Dolin would live with the Richmans, but I could see she wished they could be hers.

Nan Mary climbed farther into the wagon searching out trinkets and glass beads. The young girl's eyes sparkled like the jewelry she picked up. The pretty little thing didn't need ornaments to attract admirers, though she was only fourteen.

She scouted beyond the housewares, searching for combs to put in her golden hair. Annie had told me her second daughter wanted to live in a big city like Louisville, to walk up and down the streets. Nan Mary liked to say, "I want to see people I don't know and they don't know me."

Carrying out rakes, hoes, and dustpans from where they were propped in far corners of the wagon, Nan Mary held something behind her back.

"Guess this riddle, Mama: What has long legs, short thighs, a little head and no eyes?" Before Annie could answer, Nan Mary yelled, "Fireplace tongs!" and brought out the piece that had hips and a small head opening on a hinge.

Everyone stood spellbound as Nan Mary opened tins. Smells of cinnamon, nutmeg and brown sugar filled the air, making it seem like Christmas in a story book. She placed small packets of needles, pins, and thimbles into the hands of the others.

The peddler remarked on other sewing notions. "Perfect dress edge, not cord, not braid. Will protect. Keep skirt clean as long as skirt holds together." I handed it back to him.

"That's good percale apron, scalloped embroidery," the man said. I didn't even look close at it, just gave it to Nan Mary to return to the box where she got it. I would never buy something that Miz Annie and Grandmaw could help me make for much less cost.

Annie looked through a box of children's clothes. She held up a corduroy coat with velvet facing. "It sure would look good on Nace," she said, "but if it fit perfect now, by spring he would outgrow it."

The peddler approached softly, "You will get good wear from coat…only six dollars."

Annie put it down like it was scorching her hand.

Nan Mary handed her mother a beautiful peacock feather. It had long blue-green strips and purple circles that shined like eyes and felt like velvet. It could've belonged to a queen. Annie twirled the long, curved feather this way and that, catching sunlight.

"Oh how Christina would treasure such a pretty thing," she said softly to me.

Annie returned it to the salesman, lest he think she would buy it. He said with a hopeful voice, "Only fifty cents," but she turned away.

Foster had opened a wooden box filled with different shaped eyeglasses. He gave a pair to Annie saying, "Try these on, Mama. Maybe you can see better."

Annie held them up to her eyes, but said everything looked fuzzier than before. Same thing with another pair. The third pair had tiny sets in silver wire frames and when she put them behind her ears, her face lit up. "They fit me perfect!" She tilted her head and looked at the fat, swollen limbs of snow-covered trees in the back yard. "That snow in those branches use to look like a glob of white, and now I see branches under the snow with clumps of green straight needles sticking out. It's a miracle!"

She turned to the peddler. "How much?"

"Only two dollars, Madam." His black eyes opened wide.

Annie took off the glasses. "We can't spare the money."

Grandmaw had come out on the porch, her coat buttoned and scarf tied. She looked at the snowy steps and stayed where she was.

"You buy those!" said Grandmaw in a loud cracking voice. "Christina, run get what money is in the red jar."

"I don't want to be selfish," said Annie, but she put the glasses back on, holding them with both hands.

Grandmaw fairly waved her arms. "If Boone brings us good news about Les, we are going to do some celebrating, howdy. And you are going to want to see ever thing, for we'll be doing some high kicking."

As Grandmaw directed Christina to hand the change to the peddler, she spoke to him from the porch. "Would you take fifty-five cents and a old rooster in trade for the specs? He's not much good, and he's pretty mean, but maybe you can sell him and get your money back."

The Jewish man took off his hat and with a smile, he bowed to Grandmaw. "Madam, he will be plenty good on supper plate."

Foster chased the rooster through the snow from the barn lot and around the house. Finally, the bird tired out and dragged its claws and Foster scooped it up.

The peddler put the rooster in a cage hanging on the inside of the wagon. Then he picked up the small crate of oranges and handed it to Foster. "For good Christmas," he said, beaming.

The peddler's horse turned his head toward the children's laughing voices as they helped the man tidy his wagon. They put the copper pots inside one another, rolled wool carpets and stored them along the wagon sides. They stacked picture postcards and quilting frames. They returned calendars and cowbells, harness bells and dinner bells to cardboard boxes. Nan Mary folded clothes and laid them neatly back in their trunks.

The kids and me beamed at Annie while she turned her head back and forth and up and down. Foster smiled all time he helped the peddler close the back canvas flap, securing it with ropes.

The Jewish man picked up the peacock feather and handed it to Christina. "For happiness," he said. He gave another wide smile as he bowed, then climbed back into his wagon, ringing the bells as his horse clopped through the snow.

It wasn't snowing when the peddler man left and I took Jakie home for a rest before we headed back out. Annie said she wanted us to spend the night with them, but Christina and Dolin would be sleeping in the loft upstairs, three girls in a bed in Grandmaw's room, three more in the room with Annie and Garr, and Foster making a pallet in the kitchen. It was crazy to think they had places for us. All would be crowded up til they figgered where the new marrieds would live permanent.

There was even less room at the Linkahans. I wondered if Bertie really would marry James, her brother-in-law. It sure made sense. Lots of widowed people was almost forced to marry their dead mate's kin, especially when they had kids to raise. It also kept people from breaking one of the commandments, "Thou shalt not commit adultery." As Father Donnelly said, it covered all the sins of the flesh. He had skipped the details, only said, "Without marriage, you must keep yourself pure like the Virgin Mary."

While Jakie took a little nap, I tromped out in the snow to get extra hay for my buggy horse, to feed the Jersey cow that made such good yellow butter, and to make sure my chickens was penned up out of the snow.

The trees and the shed and the barn and chicken coop and the fences all around was covered in sparkling white, and ever thing was still and peaceful.

I thought of Les, and prayed that today the judge would decide in his favor. I could not let myself think he might be chased down to go on trial. I imagined what he would say to know that Dolin and Christina was getting married this very night.

I wished he was in front of me, lighting his cigarette and standing with his weight on one leg like he did when he was thinking. I could see him sitting at my table, his fingers touching the smooth curves of my glass preserve stand and spoon holder. I had bought it with some of my first egg-money.

I didn't need the little doo-dad, just wanted it. Something to feel good about for earning it myself. Mr. Hershall never liked things I bought. "Alls I need is flour for my biscuit and sugar for my coffee," he used to say.

The shed door was half-way open, blocked by a drift of snow.

I took a broom to sweep the opening, then stepped inside to look around. The corner was cleared out where Dolin and Cleophus had taken Mr. Hershall's stored supplies back to Rice's. In the place where the copper plate had stood, I saw the loosened edge of a wide plank.

I knelt to see if it was bare ground that needed boarding up. On looking close, I saw three wide boards was pulled loose. I prized them up and something was wedged under the floor. In the dim light of the shed, it looked like a dead animal. My heart pounded. I leaned in and what I saw was a deerskin. It was wrapped around something heavy and I used both hands to drag it through the opening. It gave a muffled jangle. What I unwrapped was a metal strongbox.

The cast iron sides had a caked-on reddish-brown powder, but the front had smooth inset panels showing fat little angels holding plates of grapes. I twisted the rusty key in the lock and the lid creaked open.

Inside the box was thick stacks of paper money—large figures— each tied with string. My fingers trembled. I had found Mr. Hershall's hidden money! I wouldn't have to worry about raising Jakie, or paying taxes, or buying feed for the stock. I could order fruit trees for a orchard and maybe look at some new store-bought dresses and a hat.

I lifted out the layers of money and uncovered a heavy pouch spread out over the bottom of the box. When I opened the drawstrings, the daylight from the door caught the shine of gold pieces. I ran my fingers through the shiny coins. I held one close to see the image of the head of Liberty with a coronet. The pouch was filled with twenty-dollar gold pieces!

Stuck in one stack of bills was a small scrap of paper. I recognized the old man's scribbling:

> To my wife Emmalene.
> Being the old man I am when you find this here is my wishes.
> The gold coin is for Les Richman as a fine man I have knowed all his life and who is not Catlick and treated me more fair then anybody. Gold is always good money and give to me by my Paw and is earned and nary any owed out.
> N Hershall

The note had no date, but I figgered Mr. Hershall had to write it sometime while Les worked at the moonshine. My mind jolted at maybe the old man had a notion of his coming death. It came to me that maybe he wished that after he was dead I'd marry Les. He would rather have Les living on his farm than anybody else.

An eerie feeling settled over me and I didn't even count the money. I laid the deer hide in the corner and lifted the strongbox. I was in a hurry and left the shed door open.

The afternoon sun made the snow blinding and I walked careful toward the kitchen door. Before I knew it, Boone rode up on his horse and I was caught between the shed and the house. He rode right up to me and got off his horse. I moved too quick and my boot slipped and Boone reached out to catch the metal box.

"Here, Emmalene, I got it," he said.

It wasn't nothing I could do but let him carry it after I had almost fell.

I opened the door and motioned for Boone to go on in.

He stepped up into the kitchen and the box gave a dull jingle. He turned and looked at me real hard, and I knew he knew what was there.

I didn't offer to say anything and he didn't ask.

"I got news," he said, grinning. "All charges is dropped against Les!"

I sat down hard in the nearest chair and my breath came in gasps. I was laughing and half sobbing together and didn't even care for Boone seeing me. His mouth twisted like he was trying not to outdo me in laughing or crying himself.

He told me he and John L. both were in the courtroom and heard it theirselves.

"I sent a telegram to Les in care of Uncle Joe, and I just now come from telling Annie and Garr and the kids. Looks like it will be a big Christmas even if Les won't be here til later when he gets the news."

Boone didn't stay long, and as he left he smiled, "Eliza told me that she has a Christmas cake for you and hopes you'll like it. She said she'd bring it to church tonight."

After I fixed Jakie a bite, I took out the money for I couldn't help counting it. First came the Double Eagles that Mr. Hershall left to Les. It was over three thousand dollars! It might take a man five, ten years or more at a good job and saving every penny to match that. I quit counting my paper money when I got to ten thousand dollars. Old Man Hershall must have saved ever cent his papa give him, plus ever spare one he made on whiskey. I stopped myself, lest I be wrong, to dream that Les and I would plan our farm and the money together.

I had looked in Boone's eyes and I was sure as if he'd promised that he would never say a word about the jingle of coins he heard. But there were others to worry about. If I took the paper money and put it in my bank account or started spending it, my business would be everybody's business. If I bought new farm tools or had a dress made, the law would come sniffing around.

I had to stop thinking that Les would take care of everything for me. And as I made plans I thought, At least I know where to start. First thing, I wanted a ledger to keep the farm books. I had enough feed for the horses to last the winter, but come spring I would have to get prices on outlay to plant oats, corn and cowpeas. The most expense would be farm workers.

Maybe when the Linkahan boys and Foster left school to put in crops at home, they could farm for me, too. They could use my farm horses to plow and haul manure from the barn to spread out over the fields and work it in. They could plant by hand. And I would need a foreman, for surely men wouldn't take orders from a woman—and supposing they did, I couldn't very well direct the work and tend to Jakie too.

And then my mind came back to Les. I felt happy and scared all at the same time. So many good things were happening for me, but troubled thoughts got in the way. I didn't know how things stood with us. There were times I believed he would go back to Maribelle, yet when he'd been drinking coffee with me, he'd said very little about her.

But that didn't mean he wasn't still taken with her.

I also couldn't be sure he cared special for me, for part of Mr. Hershall's deal with Les was me fixing supper for him every night. And Dolin had been there for him to visit. Now all was different and he had no reason to see me.

Les was free to come back and now with money, he could start his own business or do whatever he wanted. I could not let myself think that he might want to marry little Maribelle. If only he would be my husband and manage our farm.

Before starting back to the Richmans I put the coins in my dresser and the paper money under my mattress, knowing I would rest easier if it was closer to me than the shed.

I hoped I could keep my mind on anything the Richmans said, and on the Mass and the wedding, for that matter. I had just found my fortune, but I could not let anyone know. For someone had turned in Les's name and that person could turn me in for the money Mr. Hershall had left us.

Miz Annie wanted me at their house by four o'clock to see the kids find their presents from Old Santy. When Jakie and me got there, it was already a party with the excitement of Les not being charged. The walls was fairly singing with our happy shouts.

Annie had a fit over my brown suit. "Where did you get that beautiful brocaded dress and coat?"

"I found this outfit in the trunk of clothes that had been hid upstairs, and I aired it out and pressed it with a wet cloth and baking soda, and the musty smell is gone." I beamed at having something old that I made look right good.

I was glad it didn't have moth holes and was small enough to fit me. I figgered it must have been Patience Cutler Hershall's, which made it at least eighty-five years old.

Jakie wore a new coat that Grandmaw had made from leftover wool and he looked so cute in his clean shirtwaist and knickers, his big boy clothes. He kept nodding from one face to another like he knew something special was going on, but when I thought about it, he was most all time happy—ever day was Christmas for him.

We had ham and big biscuits and homemade pickles and Annie's jam cake with caramel icing, a yellow cake, and persimmons stuffed with nutmeats, rolled in sugar.

Christina got out the basket of chestnuts she and Dolin had gathered. Dolin took a ice pick and punched a couple of holes in each one so they wouldn't bust open as they filled with steam, roasting in the fireplace ashes. A kettle of dried beans hung on a S-shaped hook from the iron bar above the burning coals in the fireplace. They was cooking down with a hunk of streaked fatback and onions and some potatoes cut in long wedges, busting open and bubbling on top.

The snow fell steady outside, and from the window it was a white picture made of the trees and the barn and chicken house. Inside never seemed sweeter than being warm by the fire while looking out at the cold.

I loved the family feeling I got when we drank Annie's eggnog, with Garr playing the fiddle and all from youngest to oldest singing "O Little Town of Bethlehem."

Grandmaw said more than once, "It don't come a snow many times at Christmas, so this one is more special."

When Foster said the snow might put a hi-eetus on the wedding, Dolin spoke up loud, "We ain't putting off the wedding even if it's just Christina and me and Father Donnelly!" and the family thought it a good joke that he felt so strong about it.

The little ones' faces shined with the goodness of their life while they unwrapped paper from late fall apples and polished them. They took delight watching and listening to sparks fly up the chimney—the louder the better—for they was signs of Santy Claus, who had never forgotten them.

Around dark, Nace and Jakie woke from their sleep when the other kids came in from the snow to see that Santa Claus had been there. Under the tree was homemade rag dolls and cornshuck toys for the little girls, clay marbles for Foster and a whittled horse for Jakie. Little Nace loved his soft ball covered in felt, and hugged it to him, like it was a animal. Even down to the older folks, we each had a orange from the traveling peddler man and store-bought red and white stick candy and cinnamon drops.

Bertie and James and their family came in stamping snow and adding food to the table—plates of fried chicken, a beautiful cherry cobbler and a loaf of cinnamon bread. It took a lot of extry food, for Bertie's chaps was always hungry. Santy had already been to see them and the Richman kids compared their Christmas booty, looking over the new marbles and hoops and Cleophus' knife.

I admired Bertie's man, going to be her husband. He was dressed fine in a heavy knee-length topcoat with black leather gloves and black boots gleaming like coal. He carried a tall black hat. But he wasn't above his raisings because he joined right in with eating a slice of ever cake, and telling stories about the old days when he was a kid in Landing Run. He even went outside and brought in logs and put them in the fireplace.

Boone and Eliza soon came over to help feed the singers heading out to do the traveling minstrel show. Boone carried in fresh-cooked sausage and ribs, and Eliza's corn salad, slaw, pickled peaches, and dried apple cakes. He unpacked his wife's special sweet potato pudding and the egg custard. There would be enough eats left over to feed the singers again when they got home. And, Lord knew, there wouldn't be no shortage of whiskey nor wine for a drink with ever slice of cake.

It took a while to put out the spread, but it wasn't time for much eating or relaxing when Annie told Dolin to get some boxes down from the rafters in the attic. They was enough to outfit all that was going out—old squashed hats, ill-fitting baggy pants, and patched shirts. But Annie said not to put on no wore-out shoes. "You young people have to wear your galoshes when you go traipsing in this snow. If your feet get wet, you'll take a chill for sure."

Ever Christmastime some people made rounds of serenading in a group, dressed in shabby clothes like old-time steamboat entertainers. Some used a cork with ashes to blacken their faces like minstrels.

The neighborhood let their kids stay up to see the performers. Even if ever body had gone to bed, a loud knock with laughing, fiddle music, and bell ringing would get the household to throw open the door and invite them in.

Annie told us about her younger days. "In fair weather, us singers would walk up and down the roads and over the knobs, but in snow like tonight, we rode as far as we could and walked where the horses couldn't go."

I aimed to stay at home with Grandmaw, Miz Annie, Eliza and the youngest ones, but Bertie said, "You are way too young to stay behind; only a bit older than Christina, so you come with us and have a good time for yourself!"

Well, now Bertie is nice since she knows I'm not stealing Dolin away from her. But I had to allow that her getting security in marrying James Linkahan might have something to do with her easing up on me. And in all ways, he seemed to be a good catch.

Bertie had just told us women in the kitchen, "Sometimes I forget I was married to Wyman. I never thought so many good things about him as I do James...and he makes my blood run like sap in a young maple." Everybody laughed and she turned serious, said they married the wrong people the first time around.

James also asked me to come along. "I don't aim to wrestle around in the hay, but I am not going to miss out on all the fun. Get in the wagon with us!" I figured if he would risk his fine clothes, I could risk my best dress and coat.

Christina made a place for me to sit in the straw beside her and Dolin. We waved at Annie when she shouted after us as the horses started up with the loaded wagon. "You all be back here by ten o'clock. I don't want no laughing and drinking to make Christina and Dolin late for their own wedding!"

It wasn't long til we reached the first house. Everybody piled out and we walked up slipping and sliding. While one pounded on the door, Garr bore down on his fiddle and played "Old Joe Clark." I guess he had a drink or two, 'cause his rheumatism wasn't acting up.

Once inside, Nan Mary pulled off her galoshes and stomped her shoes to the "Buck and Wing," just like the old Scots-Irish ancestors did their jigs and clogs. Then Cleophus and Jimmy Lee took their turn. With bells on their caps and boots, they jumped in to do a "Pigeon Wing," kicking high and throwing their shoulders back, and flapping their arms like scarecrows. They held one leg up and hopped on the other, and the little kids especially, whooped and hollered at them. Some grown-ups threw pennies at their stamping feet.

At ever house, they made us sing "Oh Come All Ye Faithful" and "Angels We Have Heard On High." And the last song was always "Silent Night."

"You all have to have a piece of cake," the mother would say. And at ever stop we had to stay a bit longer for a glass of blackberry wine, or grape wine, and grape juice for the younger ones. I'm sure the man of the house along with Garr, Boone and James were having a secret swallow of moonshine.

Like Miz Annie had said before we left, "Look at them, would you? Just big ole boys!"

Les
December 1910

It was pure dark when I stepped off the train in Bardstown. Nothing seemed like Christmas Eve to me. I shook one leg then the other to unkink the cramps of sitting in the railcar all day and the night before. My throat burned from smoking so much.

I pulled my hat brim to my eyebrows and stole a look at the freight handlers. They was strangers to me.

There wasn't any moon and the falling snow dimmed the lamp beams around the station house. I watched the handlers rolling barrels and packing off cardboard boxes from the train into the stone section of the depot.

I would give a lot to already be home, where I didn't have to slink around, shielding my face from the law.

I walked, trying not to hurry, into the shadows of the station. I kept my head down and slowly looked around from under the edge of my hat, feeling like a scoundrel and afraid some fat-ass deputy would spot me and yell, "Les Richman! You're under arrest!" Then spend Christmas Eve in a dark, stinking jail cell. And who knows how long I'd be there after that.

All the familiar shapes was hid by black night or white snow. For a minute I wished it was daylight so I could see the rocky hillsides and feel more like I was home. But I quickly changed my mind, because it wouldn't take long either I'd get caught or have to hide out again on the farm in Illinois.

I drew a long breath and held it, taking stock of what laid around me. The reflecting snow disappeared against the rise of the dark knobs and hills I knew were in the distance.

I felt somebody staring at me, and I looked over at a man in a black, knee-length overcoat. I hated the cold fear racketing around my rib cage. Was it a sheriff new to Nelson County since I left? How long had I been gone? Three months, one week, I calculated.

My throat tightened as I recognized the man in the dandy clothes. Judge McPherson's son! If I knew him, he'd know me, and my goose was cooked!

He looked past me and strode over to reach out his gloved hand to a woman passenger, late departing the train steps. He pulled her close and she giggled while they hugged tight; then he led her to his shiny, black buggy.

A depot worker followed them, holding an armload of packages wrapped in silver paper and red ribbons. He put the parcels in the buggy, and then tipped his hat to the lawyer, the judge's son.

I stood by, not yet moving, and watched the woman gather up her layers of skirts and purple coat. She pulled a fur collar up close to her throat and the feathers on her big hat waved back and forth at each turn of her head.

Why does ever woman I set eyes on have dark hair and a fine figure? I fretted, as the man helped her up the step to the front seat. His horse also seemed happy to see the lady, for he wagged his head and snorted damp clouds and jerked at the reins that hitched him to the railing.

Hidden in the shadows, I scanned around the depot—from its pitched roof with pennants flying in the cold wind to the outer edge of the rail yard as far yonder as I could see. I focused in to make out a lettered sign on the small building's platform: FAST DAILY TRAINS.

Most of the passengers had left, their voices smothered in the snow cover. Only two figures straggled back onto the train, bound for somewhere south.

"Bo'oard!" the conductor's voice sang out. The train picked up speed and steamed away, and everything settled quiet.

I set out walking, seeing Christmas candles burning in windows of the closest buildings. This Christmas Eve sure was different from any other I'd spent in all my twenty-one years. Here I was coming home in the dark of night hoping old Santy Claus was making his rounds, keeping the likes of Judge McPherson or the local deputy off the streets. Although I'd have to face it sometime or other since it ain't likely the law would just forget what happened and let me come home and go my way.

I pulled the collar of my sheepskin coat up to protect my cold ears and turned west. I kicked my boots through the snow as I came into the heart of downtown Bardstown. While looking up into the elms and oaks that stood heavy with snow, a sheet of white powder blew into my face. I smiled to think how much the folks at Landing Run treasured a white Christmas—a big snow thrilled us. I thought about the women making snow cream, about hearing bells ring on the horse and sleigh, boys building snowmen and chucking snowballs at one another, and little girls taking big steps in the older ones' footprints.

Emmalene. Never far from my day and night dreams. And why hadn't I been able to tell her my heart? If I could have let her know something after Mr. Hershall died, she might have returned my feelings. But Boone said it wasn't safe to write.

I got to loving her while she was still married and taking care of Dolin's burns. But I couldn't say anything about it—couldn't betray her husband, Old Man Hershall, who had kindly give me a job working his moonshine. I just sat there at her kitchen table drinking coffee while pretending I come to see Dolin.

I threw my canvas sack over my shoulder and stepped onto the sidewalk on the east side of the main street. The place was empty, no one spilling out the doors of the saloons and pool hall. No music, no laughing or cussing. Tavern-keepers have wives that make them take off work on Christmas.

A picture of what my family'd be doing at home came to me as clear as the night air and it twisted inside me in a sweet, hurtful way.

Papa would be sawing on his fiddle, playing "Silent Night," and my half-sisters, Christina and Nan Mary, would be stringing popcorn to trim a fine cedar tree in the corner. I could see Maw Richman, sweet as a real mother to me. She'd have tears in her eyes cause she'd be so happy, and Papa'd be a teasing her about it. I reckoned they'd soon be getting ready for midnight Mass. Even Papa would go to church on Christmas Eve.

The snow-packed streets slowed me down, and I stamped my boots to kick off snow on the stone walkways at each corner. I searched the tall windows above and the awnings over the store doorways. My heart pounded when, on the roof of a low building, I saw what looked like a man holding a rifle with a bead on me.

I shook off the fear when I saw that it was a narrow chimney with a piece of metal leaning against it.

From the light of a kerosene streetlamp, I read the letters on a familiar sign: SPALDING'S DRY GOODS. Cedar boughs lined the windowsills and a great wreath with pine cones and shiny tin stars hung on the door. A placard in the largest window said, "Merry Christmas to our Patrons."

I wished the store was open so I could buy a little something to take home to Maw. Probably she'd say not to spend my money on foolishness for her, but how I'd love to see her face if I handed her a parcel of tissue paper that held a brooch for her coat lapel, or a sweet-smelling sachet for her letterbox.

Dolin's last letter that Boone handed me a month ago popped into my mind, and I moaned out loud. It was the reason I'd risked getting locked up to come home.

I can't forget the lines he scribbled in such a hurry:

> I guess you know most people here are crazy over Emmalene. Especially what all she did for me when I was burned at the sawmill. It's about time for old Santy Claus and I sure wish you could come home for all the Christmas doings. I have to sign off for Boone is waiting for it. I wish you could see me get Married before Midnight Mass the 24th. But you and me know how things is.
>
> Your friend, Dolin.

Well, no, I didn't know how things is, no matter how many times I read his letter.

I turned toward the livery stable to rent a saddle horse, as I couldn't walk five and some-odd miles to Our Lady of Hope Church before midnight. And it was sure too late to catch a ride toward Landing Run this time of night—at Christmas.

You know how things is. Dolin's words tore at me. Yes, I knew Dolin was sweet on Emmalene the first time he laid eyes on those black curls and white arms of hers. And even if she was legal married, Dolin and I both was happy the old man slept at the moonshine still and not in her bedroom. Ever body in Landing Run knew about that.

I got mad at myself, but truth was, Dolin wasn't the only one struck on Emmalene. Her blazing blue eyes. But sometimes they weren't blue. Seems like they changed color depending on the time of day. But her hair was dark. I know how it looked when some of the curls strayed out of her dust cap while she was running around the Hershall farmhouse, putting medicine on Dolin's burns, changing his bandages, laughing at my jokes while making us a pot of coffee.

My fancy of Emmalene gave me pause to question what I ever saw in Maribelle Meadors. How was I taken in with seeing her silk-stockinged ankle when she stepped into her daddy's buggy at church last spring? And after that I sat with her outside of a Sunday afternoon—her being just seventeen, a little older than Christina. I might have been thinking more serious about her if I hadn't been around Emmalene and found out the difference in feeling for a grown woman instead of a kid.

I stomped in front of the double doors to the livery stable and yelled a little too loud for the livery keeper. The man opened the window up above and his pipe smoke floated out from his warm rooms.

Candles lit up the night. Laughter and sounds of a piano drifted down to me and couples in bright clothes danced in front of a Christmas tree. I felt like crying seeing all the young people at ease, and wearing big smiles.

"This is Christmas Eve, fella!"

"I'll pay extra," I said. "For I'm in a real hurry."

The man grumbled and seemed like he took his sweet time searching out a blanket and a saddle.

He was still frowning when I handed him the money, but it was a good little horse he rented me, and she plopped sure-footed through the snow.

By the time I pulled the reins to go left at the curve headed south out Jackson Highway, I rested more easy about any big dog sheriff watching me. The heavy chimes on St. Joseph's Cathedral rang nine times. If my horse kept up a good walk I could be there in time. I would see Emmalene get married, see her eyes sparkle with how happy she was. I'd see her black hair covered in lace.

I cringed as I pictured her pressing close to Dolin and old Father Donnelly saying, "I pronounce you man and wife."

But I have to do it. I have to see that she is lost to me, that all the doors are closed. I have to let it go, for Dolin loves her too and he's a good man. And if it kills me, I'll witness it. I can't be sinking to the floor any more with my knees drawn up, grieving.

My horse could see better than I could in the dark and she followed the buggy ruts cut into the snow-packed road. Up ahead I spotted a lantern beam, and I hoped it was a friend from out Landing Run way. My mouth went dry and my hands felt weak holding the reins. If it was a neighbor, I needn't worry. They would be happy to keep mum. In fact, to all around here, it was the revenuers doing harm, trying to keep poor people from making a living in one of the few ways they could.

I drew closer. John L. Meadors stood beside his horse and buggy.

"John L., is that you?" I shouted.

"Les? Name of God, it's good to see you! How'd you get the news so quick?"

What news? I rubbed the back of my neck trying to figure what John L. meant.

I got off my horse and he clapped his gloved hand on my shoulder. "How'd you know to come home?"

Come home? Did he mean okay to come home? My mouth opened and I couldn't get enough air. I couldn't speak.

"It was noon today that Judge McPherson cleared his docket for Christmas break." John L. smiled real big. "All charges against you are dismissed!"

I felt confused, then ease spread through my body.

"Boone and me sat in the courthouse and heard it ourselves. Judge McPherson read the report from Internal Affairs about the shooting of Mr. Hershall during the raid on the moonshine. He had your name on a sheet of paper in front of him, but no one would testify that you were there." John L. slapped my shoulder, again. "His Honor banged the gavel and said, 'Case dismissed!'"

I stood there with blood rushing to my head. I felt sweat tickling under my arms.

"Boone went straight to send you a telegram at his uncle's farm, then hot-footed it home to tell Annie and them."

I imagined Maw hearing the news and throwing her apron over her eyes, her shoulders heaving. I could smell her baked ham—rubbed with sugar and scored with cloves—and roasted sweet potatoes. And I could see her best dishes sparkling in the candlelight and taste the tang of Papa's homemade wine. Christina and Nan Mary would be putting icing on a couple of big cakes, and all the little kids would be yelling and running around the kitchen table, excited about me coming home and all the feasting and what Old Santy would bring.

I wasn't sure I could yet talk. Or walk. So I stood there for a minute. It had started to snow again and I brushed the powdery flakes off my horse's mane.

"That's good news," I finally said with a break in my voice. I felt a smile spread over my face. I bent down and scooped up a snowball and threw it at the stiff, still trees lining the right side of the road.

John L. said, "We bought things for Maribelle and Retta, then had big Christmas doings in town with some people that do business with me. It was late when we got on the road and headed for Midnight Mass, and then the wheel started in to clattering and wobbling."

Relieved as I was to find out my good fortune, I thought about this trouble making me late. But there was nothing to do but help.

"I think the axle is about to break," said John L.

As I bent to look at the rear wheel my eye caught a flash of skirts and petticoats jumping down from the buggy steps. Maribelle. I hoped she didn't see me frown.

"Oh, Les! You've come to save us! We might have frozen to death," she cried.

What a child she is, always making a big show.

From the front seat, the girl's mother, Retta, climbed out. "Maribelle, don't walk in that snow! You'll get your feet wet and ruin your new shoes. I told you to wear your rubbers."

"Mama, they're so ugly!"

It surprised me how I wished they'd both shut up. I turned to John

L. "Set that lantern close and let's take a look."

John L. lifted the edge of the buggy frame and I twisted off the wheel. The axle clip had worn in two.

"It's a good thing you stopped before it flung the buggy ever which away," I said. "You got anything in that gear kit?"

"I can't find a regular clip, but I got a couple perch pins. You think they'll work?"

I took the box and rummaged through the metal washers, lynch pins and boxings. I found some pieces that would fix the wheel and opened the can of axle grease. I had nothing to dip it with, but my bare hands was already greasy so I grabbed a handful of gunk and spread it over the axle.

I was determined to go to the church, but I hated to go in the building smelling like oil. I reckoned it didn't matter anyway. I wasn't aiming to get near Emmalene.

Ain't this the way of it? I find out I'm free to come home and I feel real good about it, and then it kills my soul when I think of the wedding that will be going on in less than an hour.

My hands grew numb working with the cold parts while Maribelle stood over my shoulder.

"I hope we won't be late for church," she said. "I bought a fringed shawl in Bardstown and for a while there, I thought I wasn't going to get to show off my Christmas clothes."

I frowned and sniffed but couldn't take time to find my handkerchief.

Maribelle stooped down closer to me, her skirts dragging in the snow. What now?

"I got something to tell you," she whispered.

I didn't pay much attention to what she was saying. I wasn't going to leave them stranded, but I kept worrying about how late it was getting—surely close to midnight.

"Lift that buggy," I said to John L., and I fitted and shoved the wheel back on the axle.

Maribelle said under her breath, "Since I'll be boarding at the college, I wouldn't get to see you anyway."

What the deuce was she talking about?

"I really hate to break your heart like this," she said in a little voice.

I searched my memory for how I left things with Maribelle after the moonshine raid. Did I see her before I left? Had I said anything about coming back to her? Did I ever say I cared that much about her?

As I slid the clip in place on the wheel, I looked up at Maribelle. She shook her curls and had such a sad look, I wanted to laugh.

John L. packed up the box of tools and spare parts, throwing them in the boot of the buggy. He walked up close to me and turned his back to his wife and daughter who were climbing into the buggy. I thought it was about Maribelle's whisperings. Was he going to hold me to marrying her to keep her home instead of going off to school?

"Don't be mad at her, Les, but early on, Maribelle, not thinking, said something to her dressmaker in Bardstown about you working at the shine. And the wife of Judge McPherson's son was in the shop and she told your name to somebody else who told it to Sheriff Winters."

I wiped my hands on a old work rag and scuffed my boot back and forth in the snow.

John L.'s eyebrows were pulled tight. "Maribelle didn't mean you no harm, and as it happened, nobody would back up what Winters said, so he's the one that's lucky they didn't go further into Mr. Hershall getting killed."

I stared at the snowy road, then took a breath and looked up. "I don't fault Maribelle," I said. I didn't want bad blood with John L., who had always been good to me. To myself I thought, Silly, stupid girl!

John L. shook my hand with both of his. "Les, you are an ace worker and as fine a man as I know. If you ever want the job, I'd be proud to have you back to work at the sawmill and I'd make you the manager."

I looked at him and was about to speak, but he patted my arm. "Now, don't make up your mind right now. Just think on it."

He climbed up to the driver's seat and the women waved. Retta leaned her head out. "Les, thanks ever so much for stopping to give us a hand. I guess we'd all better hurry, now. You sure don't want to miss seeing your sister get married!"

Wait a minute! My sister? What about Emmalene? I wondered if I was still asleep on the train. I couldn't take it all in. Was it Christina getting married and not Emmalene?

Maribelle leaned her head in front of her mother, saying something about how excited Christina was to be marrying Dolin.

I didn't want to let on that I had thought Emmalene was the bride. I wanted to read Dolin's letter again. Was Christina's name mentioned?

My horse pawed the crusted snow in the road, eager to be off. I wanted to race ahead of John L.'s buggy, but I held myself in check. It wouldn't do to hurt my good little horse just because I was flying high.

I bounced in the saddle, hardly knew where I was, and directly I saw the twinkle of lanterns up ahead. Church bells rang out across the snow, calling the people together.

Christmas! I thought of Emmalene and home and all the cookies and mistletoe, our family sitting around the fireplace, singing. I wanted to hang on to this powerful good feeling and hope for it in later Christmases, yet I knew nothing would ever again be as sweet as this one.

Emmalene
December 1910

By ten-thirty, all the Richmans and me were ready to go to church—Christina into her wedding suit and the kids into their good clothes. Dolin went across the knob to the Linkahans to ride to church with them. Miz Annie had let Jakie and little Nace stay asleep til we were all piling into the wagon. Even Garr, who never went to church, combed his hair nice and put on his only suit coat. This special night was for midnight Mass, but more important to the Richmans and Linkahans, just after the church bells rang twelve, Christina and Dolin would be married.

Miz Annie said, "I won't take no for a answer."

So Jakie and me sat in the front pew of the church with Christina and the older Richmans, while the rest of the kids sat in the pew behind us.

I opened the leather-bound missal Father Donnelly had gave me for learning my catechism so good. He told me I had a true devotion. I wasn't sure of that, but I liked it when he said, "Converts enlightened by divine grace make the best Catholics, and I believe you know more about the faith than most of the people at Our Lady of Hope."

Father said by Easter I could be taking the first sacraments of Baptism, Confession, and Communion.

I often pondered what my mother would think about me studying up on what Catholics believe, yet I knew what she would say: "You have a good mind, Child, and also a good heart. Use them both and you will do what is right."

And what would Les think? If I converted it shouldn't bother him. His papa wasn't a Catholic although he married one. And they had a lot of kids and seemed to work everything out.

But yet, Les shouldn't care if I didn't get baptized either since he never did—that is if he cared at all what I did.

Ever since I found Mr. Hershall's money, my mind and heart were at war. I had more riches and property than most in Landing Run, and I didn't have to marry anybody. I could take care of Jakie and buy what I needed without any help from any Catholics.

But that sounded like something Mr. Hershall would say. It was true, I wanted the friendship of the neighbors, but it was Les I wanted to be with ever day, Les I felt at home with, Les who stirred my heart and body.

Once while Dolin was burned and staying at the house, Mr. Hershall had asked Les to take my horse out for exercise. The old man had not looked at me, just nodded in my direction and snarled, "She can't do it. She's too busy taking care of strangers."

That night after Les brought my horse back to the barn, I'd walked in. Les had the currying brush going in long sweeps over the horse's back and belly. I heard him talking soft, "Easy, there, Pretty Girl, this'll make you feel good."

I watched my horse lean into the brush as Les moved the bristles gently on its underbelly. "Oh, you like that, don't you?" he said. The horse flicked its ears back and forth and made deep, lippy noises. "Let me do that some more," Les said. And I watched my horse's skin shudder. Then she relaxed her neck and let her head fall forward.

My mind came back to church when I saw Father Donnelly standing in the door of the sanctuary, waiting for the choir to finish its songs. In celebration of Christmas, he wore white satin vestments and all the purple altar cloths of Advent were folded away. The choir didn't have music but that made the words all the sweeter. They sang "It Came Upon A Midnight Clear," and Miz Annie squeezed my hand. I know she was thinking not only about her daughter about to be married, but also that Les would soon come home.

It was already planned that when the choir sang "Silent Night," Christina would stand up and walk from her pew to the center aisle and Dolin would come from the pew opposite and take her arm. They would walk together to stand in front of the priest.

Annie leaned over and whispered, "Retta and John L. aren't here yet. Would you go to the door and see if they're on their way?"

I slipped out the side aisle passing the smiling faces of Eliza and Boone. From across the church, Bertie gave me a big grin, and nodded her head at me. She had on a new red velvet suit and a big new hat and was sitting close to James. His short beard touched with silver showed up splendid against his dark-vested suit, and he sat like a gentleman with his shoulders back. Then he turned all cuddly when Baby Wyman crawled into his lap and up on his shoulder to grab his snowy white collar.

All the Linkahan boys had on new Christmas duds and filled the pew around their mother and James. I figured James had bought new clothes for the whole family. Bertie looked as happy as Christina, and I reckoned she was going to marry James pretty soon.

At the back, I pushed open the door into the cold night air. In the faint light coming from the candlelit windows, I could see a line of rigs tied to the rail. A hound dog yipped and sniffed along the row of horses, then circled away.

Through the soft falling snowflakes I made out Retta and Maribelle hurrying along the snow-covered walkway. As they reached me waiting on the stoop, Maribelle lifted her skirts, and I noticed the edges below the double ruffle were damp and soiled. In the darkness behind them, John L. tied his buggy horse to the rail.

"Oh, Emmalene, has anything started yet?" Maribelle sang out. With her free hand, she patted a big, round hat, sitting high on her stacked mounds of hair. A velvet purse slid up and caught on her long-buttoned gloves.

Retta said a quick hello then turned back to hurry John L. along. "Come on! They won't hold up things forever."

John L. looked behind him at the shadows in the churchyard but kept moving forward. He took off his hat, nodded to me and followed his wife and daughter into church.

Something about the slow movements of a person in the shadows looked familiar. I watched the man rub his horse with a heavy cloth, then throw a blanket over its back. He bent down, scooped up snow and rubbed his hands together as if to clean them.

I thought I must be seeing things when the figure in the sheepskin jacket walked toward me. Les!

My body trembled but I couldn't move my legs. As I watched, Les took off his hat, jammed it in his pocket, and took giant steps to me. I smelled farm machinery and tobacco as I leaned toward him and he caught me in his arms. I felt the stubble of his beard on my face and his low broken voice, "Emmalene, Emmalene."

I remembered his lips as looking tense, tightly pressed together, but when he kissed me, his lips were forceful and still gentle. He couldn't take his mouth off mine for a long time.

"My hands are dirty," he said, but I stopped his talk with another kiss. I tilted my head up and saw what I longed for—a wanting, pleading look in his eyes. He opened his coat and pulled me close, and I thrilled to hear him breathe in my ear, "I couldn't stand the thought of you being anybody's wife but mine!"

The church bells began striking midnight and the choir started singing "Silent Night."

Yellow light from the church window reflected against the dancing flakes—a sprinkling of fairy gold dust. I opened the door and drew Les inside. People turned around and smiled and a low buzz filled the church. "It's Les!" "Les Richman is home!"

From the front pew, Miz Annie stood beaming at us, and she took off her new glasses to wipe her eyes. Christina and Dolin paused before walking toward the altar. When they saw it was Les who had come in, their faces were all lit up and they waved. Then they turned and walked arm and arm to say their vows in front of Father Donnelly.

I knew I must cut short my moment with Les, to give him up to the joy of his sister's wedding and the welcome home from the community. I touched his arm, and he pulled me close to his side. He whispered a one-word question, "Emmalene?"

I answered, "Yes, yes, yes."

Acknowledgements

This book, under the title *Landing Run* was available for a time on Amazon Kindle, 2012.

An excerpt from a chapter previously titled "The Wake," appeared in Nancy Gall-Clayton's course packet for Jefferson County Community College.

A chapter in a different form titled "The Peddler's Visit" was published in a literary journal, *Arable, #3*, and also appeared in another variation as a short story, "Christmas Peddler," in the anthology *Christmas is a Season: 2008*.

A chapter in a slightly different form titled "Home for Christmas: Bardstown, Kentucky, 1910" was published in the anthology *Christmas is a Season: 2009*.

Portions of the manuscript were aired on Central Kentucky Radio Eye, Inc., 2012-2013.

A love of family and their stories inspired and encouraged me to write about the real community of Landing Run. Although I have fictionalized the events and characters, it is my hope that I have represented the lives and values of the people who lived in that rural area of Kentucky in 1910.

I am most appreciative of loving, supportive parents, Gerald and Helen Rogers; my siblings, Ruth Ann, Gary, Wanda, Linda, Dinnie and Elizabeth; my daughters Mary Jo Gediman and Laura Pfannmoeller, sons-in-law Dan Gediman and Mark Pfannmoeller, and to my special friend and confidante, Maggie Wise Riley.

I am grateful for memories and comments shared by other family members, especially Aunt Lula Rogers, Aunt Bessie Cecil, Aunt Ruth Greenwell, Aunt Addie Everhart, Marcella Downs, Libby Daniels, Leora Doyle, Warren Greenwell, Jimmy Ball, Rickey Ball, Scarlett Stokes and Jamie Arroway.

I give credit for superb guidance to learn the craft of writing to my mentors in Spalding University's MFA in writing program: Sena Jeter Naslund, Roy Hoffman, Connie May Fowler, Robin Lippincott and Phil Condon. I give a salute to the many workshop leaders who critiqued portions of the manuscript: Melissa Pritchard, Julie Brickman, Wesley Brown, Kirby Gann, Dianne Aprile, Neela Vaswani and Mary Clyde; and to fellow students' generous help: David Hassler, Kathleen Thompson, Linda Parker, Pam Sexton, Matt Jaeger, Cate McGowan, Charlotte Dixon, Deidre Woollard, Crystal Wilkinson, Molly MacDonald, Bobbi Buchanan, Diana Raab, Heather Shaw, O'Donnell Lee, Sue Carls, Troy Ehlers, Sharon Full, Andrew Beahrs, Jim Robertson, Amy Clark, Dawn Shamp, M. Kay Miller, Mike Hampton, Kelly Parisi and Vicki Weaver.

I give thanks to my writers' groups—my long-standing friends in my beloved Cherokee Roundtable, most of whom have heard me read each portion of the manuscript and especially those who read it in entirety: Jerry Lee Rodgers, Bill Lively, Wils Murphy and Denise Tanner; the Java Scribes: Anne Axton, Allison Jones, Jan Mattingly Weintraub, Katy Yocom, Kimberly Garts Crum, Susan Treitz, Thelma Wyland, Holly Brockman Johnson, Leslie Townsend, Beth Adler and Nicole Brown; to the AM Writers: John Boyd, Beverly Giammara and Heidi Saunders; and The Friday Group.

Special thanks for long-time or long-ago support and advice: Nancy Gall-Clayton, Selma Jacob, Ron Rubin, Jeff Wade, Kim Michele Richardson, Al Wagner, John Tomlinson, Karen Mann, Kathleen Driskell, Lucy Pritchett, Dixie Hibbs, Julia Strange, Charlotte Selman, David Hall, Lucy Freibert, John Filiatreau and Margaret Thornsberry Hagan.

I cannot express the depth of appreciation and love for my best friend, my comfort and joy, my soulmate, my husband, Ronnie Popham.

CPSIA information can be obtained at www.ICGtesting.com
Printed in the USA
LVOW06s1959110314

376909LV00003B/61/P